Lynette Wonders about Sex in Her Twilight Years

Lynette Wonders about Sex in Her Twilight Years

Mary E. Schumacher

Copyright © 2009 by Mary E. Schumacher.

Library of Congress Control Number: 2009906390
ISBN: Hardcover   978-1-4415-5032-3
               Softcover   978-1-4415-5031-6

All rights reserved. No part of this book may be reproduced or transmitted in any form or by any means, electronic or mechanical, including photocopying, recording, or by any information storage and retrieval system, without permission in writing from the copyright owner.

This is a work of fiction. Names, characters, places and incidents either are the product of the author's imagination or are used fictitiously, and any resemblance to any actual persons, living or dead, events, or locales is entirely coincidental.

This book was printed in the United States of America.

To order additional copies of this book, contact:
Xlibris Corporation
1-888-795-4274
www.Xlibris.com
Orders@Xlibris.com
60305

To my children: Brenda Schumacher Doherty, Lorraine Schumacher Concilio, Ed Otto Schumacher, and Robert Roy Schumacher

Acknowledgment

A special thanks to my daughter Brenda who bought me a new computer.

A special thanks to my daughter Lorraine who helped me with the computer.

I want to acknowledge my pen pal, Barbara Lynch, who uncomplainingly edited every page of the book.

Mary E. Schumacher also wrote *I Promise You Emma Mae: A Family Story*.

This book is a work of fiction. Names, characters, places, and incidents are the product of the author's imagination. Facts may or may not have been used fictitiously. Any resemblance to actual persons, living or dead, is coincidental.

Chapter 1

Lynette stood stark naked in her bathroom staring at her image in the full-length three-way mirror. Now in her early seventies, it was no longer her youthful body looking back at her. Her nude body showed operation scars, with skin rolls and folds of fat tissue. She chuckled to herself about the expression "If you can pinch more than an inch of fat, you need to lose weight." *Hah, what about three inches to pinch? Does that make you obese?* Since starting her diet, she had lost forty pounds. *Only twenty more pounds to lose*, she thought, *and I will have the body for someone to see without feeling embarrassed.* Lynette did not realize she looked good even without clothing. *Will there ever again be sex or a lover in my life?* she wondered. *I do not belong to any clubs. I do not hang out at bars. How or where will I find him? Or will he just walk up to my door?*

Lynette did have a buddy, Belinda, who used to be her next-door neighbor; Belinda never worked or married. She stayed home caring for her parents who died within a year of each other. Her father had always taken care of the family's finances; Belinda had never known how much in debt they were. After her father passed away, she put their house up for sale. To have a steady flow of income, she asked Lynette if she could work as a caregiver for Tony.

When Lynette moved to Maplewood, Florida, her companion, Tony, was suffering from brain dementia, and she needed someone to help take care of him, especially on days of her medical appointments. How wonderful Lynette felt having a caregiver living next door. Lynette and Belinda became friends. Belinda sold her family home one year before Tony had passed away. She was now renting a one-bedroom condo at the end of Oak Lane.

About two years after Tony died, Belinda was hired as a caregiver for a small assisted-living family home. It was hard work, but Belinda was in her late fifties with no experience and needed this job. She felt obligated to go to work whenever she was asked, even on her days off, for fear of losing her job.

It was at her place of work that she met a man in his sixties who was in charge of the maintenance department. They hit it off good. Lynette was happy for Belinda; however, there was little time left for just the two of them. *Oh well, that is life,* Lynette thought.

Lynette enjoyed taking bubble baths but had fallen recently. She had a shower installed in the bathroom because there was not enough room for a modern large tub. Today, after taking a shower, she closed her eyes and let her imagination take over her mind and body, as she had done so many times before. He was standing in the doorway of the bathroom as she stepped out of the shower. He stood there staring admiringly at her naked body while holding the bath towel in his hands ready to dry off her back. She walked slowly toward him. They hugged; she let him kiss her forehead, a kiss on each cheek, another kiss on her soft lips. Her body leaned back as he kissed her throat. She felt her knees go weak. Her emotions were quivering; she felt moistness between her legs. She lowered her arms from his shoulder to his waist. Quickly, she unbuckled his belt; without looking, her fingers unzipped the zipper, and with a swift nudge of her hands, his loose jeans slid to his ankles. Her eyes looked downward, taking in the fact he wore no underwear. She wet her lips as she let her hands caress his well-endowed penis.

Lynette was now at the point where her imagination always slipped back to reality with a trembling pulse throbbing in her groin. *Why can't this be real?* she wondered. *Or at least, be long enough to bring me to a climax!* With a sigh, she turned her attention to her plans for the day.

She would go to the Eggs Your Way Restaurant, which served eggs all day along with a normal menu. The waitresses all knew what Lynette wanted to eat at all her meals without her ordering from the menu. Everyone knew she was alone, and they would greet each other as friends. Sometimes a waitress or the owner would sit at her table, sipping coffee and chatting up a storm for a few minutes about nothing of any importance, yet feeling they had just shared a great conversation. After leaving the restaurant, Lynette would take care of all her errands. Later she would return home and watch TV and maybe do some chores in her house or backyard. Perhaps she would ride the three-wheeled bike or walk with poles for thirty minutes. Lynette loved swimming in her pool, finding excuses to sunbathe on the various lounge chairs and read a book. Most of these activities involved staying in her fenced-in yard.

Lynette thought of going to the beach. It was the best and the cleanest beach on the gulf in Florida's entire coastline; Lynette truly loved walking on this sandy beach but refused to go there alone. And she was a true soap opera fan. Even her medical appointments had to be scheduled before two or after three, just so she could watch the TV show of *As the World Turns*. These actors were, in a special way, her best friends. Not the actors themselves but the ones they played on the show. She had been watching this show before President Jack Kennedy was shot. Again, Lynette thought, *How in the world will I ever meet the man of my dreams if I don't make the effort to leave my house, yard, or pool? Maybe it is time to start doing some volunteering or finding a job or, at least, joining a club.*

She began dressing. She could now fit into a pair of white Levi's jeans with the cutoff legs, making them into shorts. She was deliriously happy. Just a few weeks ago, she could not pull them up over her thighs, let alone zip them. All her tank tops were now too loose; however, she still wore them with a wide belt at the waist and a long-sleeve blouse over them. Her shorts were just tight enough to fit snuggly over her rounded rear end. Today she felt sexy and walked in that confident way, which would arouse any male giving her a second look.

After breakfast, she went to the nearby Wal-Mart store, where she wandered aimlessly up and down the aisles, stopping at the jewelry department. Sally appeared to be taking some kind of inventory. As Lynette admired the rings, she thought back to the previous week. Her daughter Joyce from New Jersey had visited her for a long weekend. During that time, they had looked at rings at this very jewelry counter. Sally had chatted with them about a few rings in the safe, which had been discounted that morning.

"We're not interested in buying any jewelry, we're only looking," Joyce said. Sally, however, displayed a few small envelopes with rings. Lynette's eyes sparkled with delight as she saw and tried on a pale green gemstone ring. "I've never seen an emerald look like that before," she said.

"It's not an emerald," Sally explained. "It's a peridot, another rare gem." Lynette closed her ears to what was said. She was only interested in how beautiful the ring shone on her finger. It was on sale big-time. She wanted to buy the ring now. She could put it on her credit card, which was not maxed out yet.

Sally sighed, and smiling, she whispered, "Don't be in a hurry. Jewelry is like a man, he must be very attractive to you and chosen carefully to last a long time. Don't settle for the first one that you look at. Come to the end of this counter. There is a ruby ring that has been marked down even more than the peridot ring you're spinning your head at."

Lynette laughed, "I know there are pretty trinkets at your counter, but tell me where're these men we can choose from?" Joyce gave her mother a disconcerting look while nudging her mother's shoulder; then, with a nod of Joyce's head, Lynette knew to follow them both to the end of the counter, not that it would change her thoughts one iota about the ring she was wearing.

Sally was true to her word. The ring was fantastic, to say the least. The ring had a large ruby in the center with diamond-shaped sapphires going around the ruby. Lynette removed the green ring quickly and slipped on the ruby ring.

"I want this ruby ring. I don't want the green ring!"

"Are you sure?"

"Oh, Joyce, when have you ever seen a more dazzling ring? The other ring is pretty, but this one is divine!"

"Okay! Mother, I will buy the other ring, if you really don't want it," Joyce said firmly. For a moment, Lynette wondered if she could afford to buy them both. What was she thinking? She would let Joyce have the green ring that she calls a peridot. Lynette stared at her finger with the ruby ring on it. This was the most beautiful ring she had ever seen. What other ring could light up her hand and probably could be seen at a distance.

"Joyce, if you want that ring, it is yours," said Lynette.

There were a few customers waiting for Sally to finish the sale. Lynette suggested Sally take care of the nearest gent wanting only to change his watch battery if she had one his size. Sally paid no attention to what Lynette had said. Joyce whispered, "Sally has a big sale of hundreds of dollars. There is no reason in hell that she should stop and change his three-dollar battery." Lynette was wearing her ruby ring. Joyce's ring needed to be sized. Lynette would pick it up in a few days and mail the ring to Joyce by UPS. Today Lynette was still wearing her new ruby ring. Joyce had returned to New Jersey without her ring; Lynette would ask Sally if it was ready. She looked up and saw Sally hurrying toward her.

"The ring is not here," Sally said, "but I am glad to see you today."

Lynette was puzzled. "I know I am early, but I always stop and take a gander at your merchandize. When will my daughter's ring be ready? I don't want Joyce to think I am wearing her ring."

Sally took a deep breath in and let it out quickly. "Like I said before, the ring is not here yet but on its way. There was a problem at the warehouse where all the rings are sized. I made a mistake and sent the ring to the custom department. They returned the ring to my department. I found the ring, which was not sized, in the safe and have forwarded the ring where I should have sent it in the first place. Forgive me." Sally took another deep breath this time let it out slowly. "Do you remember the man who needed his battery changed on his watch?" Lynette thought, *Yes, I remember the man, he was very patient.* Blushing, Lynette replied, "Vaguely." Sally's voice was now almost a whisper as she said, "While he waited to have his watch battery changed, he overheard you and your daughter talking. He left his phone number. If you are interested, give him a call. I can vouch for him. A real nice guy, he is my neighbor."

Lynette wanted to take the piece of paper with the telephone number written on it but did not want to appear to be eager. Instead, as she walked away, Lynette said, "Guess he missed his big chance. He should have followed us." Just then, Lynette felt a warm heavy hand on her right shoulder. She was startled. It was the man needing the watch battery the previous week. She gave him an inquiring look. He reached out his right hand to her. Automatically, Lynette shook his hand.

Sally waved to them. "Okay, I have done my part with you two. Go have a cup of coffee at McDonald's. I have to get back to my work."

He asked, "How about a McDonald's breakfast? I have a couple of bucks. If we hurry, we can make it before they stop serving breakfast." Lynette nodded her head. They hurried to the McDonald's in the same store. They each ordered. "Put it on one bill," he told the cashier. Turning to Lynette, he explained that would be faster. Lynette paid the bill while he found a table in the far corner where they could eat and talk to their hearts' content without bothering anyone.

"I'm Chester Givens," he said. "I'm divorced, with one daughter who is married to a soldier. She is living in Rolland. That's the next town over from Maplewood."

She nodded and introduced herself. "I'm divorced too. I was married for almost thirty years, most of them unhappy. Then I had a companion for twenty years until his death. I have three children, but the only one in Florida is a daughter, and she lives an hour away. Do you live around here?"

"Actually I live in Gary, Indiana, but I am renting a condo on Venice Island for the winter months. And I am still single because I haven't met any interesting women, until now."

Lynette felt herself blush at the compliment. She had been alone for a few years and only recently had started thinking about men again. She hoped her face wasn't as red as his hair. Surely, that fire red color came from a bottle. She colored her hair, so why shouldn't he? *It looks awful*, she thought. *Why hasn't his daughter told him?* If they became a couple, she would help him tone it down.

She sipped coffee as she thought about his good traits. Like her, he was in his early seventies. And he was a few inches taller than she. Where she was loud, he was so soft-spoken he seemed to be whispering. She had always been drawn to overbearing, dominating men, but Chester had an easy way about him that touched her heart. Yes, he was someone she wanted to know better.

Chester had written something on a piece of paper and handed it to her. "This is my phone number," he said. "And what is yours?"

After she told him, he asked, "And your address?"

"Call me!" Lynette answered, "You have my number." She was surprised when she heard herself say, "I would like to know you better." She blushed, lowered her head, and said, "I will be free Friday. Give me a call."

Chester kept his arm draped over Lynette's shoulder as they slowly walked to her car in silence. He stood so close to her she could almost feel his heart beat. She felt an urge to hug him right there and didn't care who saw them; however, Chester stepped back about a foot or so from her, as if he could read her mind.

He wore his short-sleeve shirt unbuttoned at the neck, and she noticed a scar. They started talking again, giving out more information about their past lives.

Lynette could not help herself as she reached over and softly touched the scar. Their eyes met; Chester took her hand from his chest and lightly kissed her fingers. He said, "I will tell you about that another time."

"I . . . I am sorry," she stammered.

Chester opened his wallet and took out a photo. Turning it over, he asked, "Do you have a pen? I seem to have lost mine." She opened the flap of her purse and withdrew a huge pen. Laughing, he took the pen saying, "You could not lose this pen if you tried. I want to write down your license plate number. There are a lot of tan Century Buicks in the area. My car is on the other side of the parking lot. It is a blue Chevy Impala."

Lynette didn't want the conversation to be over. She didn't want to say good-bye. There was an awkward moment or two as she waited to see if he would shake her hand or lightly kiss her. Chester merely touched her shoulder, and with a nod, he left her as she unlocked her car door.

Chapter 2

No sooner had Lynette walked into her house when the phone rang. Caller ID told her it was her friend Belinda.

"Hello, my friend," said Lynette. Belinda replied into the phone, "It is me! I want to go to the beach tomorrow morning. Want to go with me?"

"Yes!"

"You have to be ready to walk out your door at seven."

"I can do that!" A few more words were spoken about each other's day; Lynette smiled as she hung up the phone. *I am going to the beach tomorrow and collect shells*, thought Lynette as she danced around the room.

The next morning, Lynette was up at five and ready at six. There still was another hour to kill, so she did her chores, including hanging the washed clothes on the clothesline in the backyard. It was almost seven when the phone rang. It was Belinda. She had received a call from work and needed to fill in for a coworker who did not come in. *Damn*, thought Lynette. She had really looked forward to going to the beach. Maybe Belinda was right. She was dressed, so there was no reason to stay home. She would go at least once; she didn't have to stay if she didn't want to. If she enjoyed herself, she could do it more often.

Lynette thought about how often she had wanted to go to the beach with Tony, but she had pustular psoriasis and was not comfortable with the skin sores on her arms and legs. The psoriasis had attacked her fingers, which were inflamed, and her nails were crumbled and filled with pus. Wherever she went, she always covered up completely, even wore white cotton gloves.

Belinda had tried to push Lynette into the social activities at the church, but Lynette was embarrassed by her skin sores. She stayed home willingly, only went wherever Tony had to go. Lynette's neighbors had voiced their opinion about the psoriasis, which they said was caused by stress; if Lynette was more sociable and less stressed out about Tony, her skin would clear up. Tony was in his demented state of mind for six years. After Tony passed away from a massive heart attack, Lynette's skin did heal, except for the nail beds on her fingers; they still had no nails, but the sores were becoming less noticeable.

Maybe she should go out into the world; start now by going to the beach today, there was no time like the present. She would be wearing her old shorts, blending with all the other beachgoers.

Lynette drove the two miles, parking in the lot nearest the beach. Only a few cars were in the lot. She walked on the sandy footpath to where the soft waves slowly crashed along the sandy shore. Lynette noticed there were only a handful of beach walkers who were collecting seashells as she was prepared to do herself. Holding her net bag, she walked past a few men fishing. No one bothered her.

She felt good when a beachcomber greeted her with a hello or good morning. Lynette saw in a distance a group of four trees. She planned to walk only that far, then turn back, and fill her bag with shells of any kind and size, hoping to find an eye-catching seashell like the ones she had found several years ago on Clearwater Beach with Tony.

As she walked toward her goal, Lynette noticed a big boulder with a man sitting on it. Lynette could not keep herself from staring at him. He greeted her with a big friendly smile as he hollered, "Good morning!" Lynette's face brightened up. She waved to him. "Instead of sitting there, come join me collecting shells," she said.

He came stumping in the sand toward her; Lynette kept on walking slowly with an occasional backward glance at him, smiling to herself. When he caught up with Lynette, she noticed he was tall enough that she had to look up to him. His salt-and-pepper hair was combed, yet windblown a bit. He was so average looking, and cheerful, that Lynnette felt she had known him all her life. "If you had a bag, you could help me with my shell gathering," she said.

He shook his head, "Sorry, next time you should bring an extra bag. You walk so very slow. My long legs have trouble staying in step with you."

Happily, they chatted as they walked till they came to the group of trees; Lynette stopped. "Here is where I turn around and walk back trying to fill this bag at least half full. Are you coming with me?"

He stared at her for a moment, shaking his head. "Nope! This is where we part company. I am walking further on."

Sadly, she walked collecting seashells until her bag was half full and quite heavy. Lynette now only picked up an eye-catching but small seashell. When Lynette looked back, he was not even a shadow. She wondered, *Why didn't we introduce ourselves, or talk about where we lived or our life, like Chester and I did. Oh well, he probably is married with a bunch of kids, or has a girlfriend lying on a beach blanket, or at home waiting for him to return. We are nothing but true beachcombers. He is a walker, and I am collecting seashells. What am I trying to do? Hash something into two strangers, walking on the beach, being friendly?*

At home, she hosed the shells and placed them around a tree in the front yard. *Looks like I need more shells, lots more shells. Yes, I will have to go back for more shells. I wonder if I'll see my smiling beachcomber again.* Lynette blushed as she wondered what he thought of her. Did he think she was too forward?

It was almost one in the afternoon, and Lynette was glad to lie on the couch for an hour before her TV program came on. She practically jumped off the couch when the front doorbell rang. "I will be right there," she hollered. Standing outside the screened door stood Chester, grinning. "My goodness, this is a surprise. How did you know where I live? I didn't tell you," said Lynette.

Sheepishly, he answered, "I went on the Internet." Lynette waved her arms welcoming Chester in the door. "You do know today is only Thursday? Well, you are here now. Come in!" Chester leaned toward Lynette, giving her a hug and a kiss on the forehead. *I better keep moving with this guy,* Lynette thought, *for I am picking up his body signals that are causing me to want to undress him. Good grief, I must slow down. I don't really know him.* Lynette took his hand. "Let me give you the tour of my house, the backyard, and pool." This was something she proudly showed all her visitors. Lynette took Chester's hand as they slowly walked on a white concrete path, which went around the cage of the pool and patio. Every ten feet or so, alongside the concrete path, there was either a concrete or wood bench where Lynette sat with Tony, as they walked many times around the pool cage, being careful to stay on the concrete path. She was pointing at the various sheds and was about to explain why there were the red and yellow bricks in the yard going from the white fence to the white path when she heard. "Hey, you have a lot of benches!"

"Yeah, I needed them when I walked Tony around the yard. He would tire quickly, and I needed a place where we could sit and rest, without both of us falling down. How on earth would I be able to raise him up from the ground by myself?"

Chester pulled her to his chest, giving her a hug, and placed his hand on her rear end, gently pressing her body closer to him. Without realizing what was happening, her body reacted by arching her back, bringing the groin area of her body tight against his lower body. She came to her senses upon feeling his hard penis pressing against her thigh. Lynette shook her head smiling and pushed him at arm's distance away from her.

A big grin softened his face. "What is the matter?" Lynette started to laugh softly. "I think you are moving a little too fast for me," she replied. Taking his arm, she said, "Let's go inside, and I can make you coffee."

Chester walked alongside Lynette with his hand gently rubbing her shoulder, then slowly sliding to her back. *If he could make me this jumpy with just a hand resting on my shoulders*, she thought, *imagine what he could do if we went to bed.* Chester broke into her thoughts as he said, "Forget the coffee. Want to go out for lunch?" Lynette firmly said, "Another time. My TV program is about to go on. In fact, it has been on for a half an hour, which means it is time for you to go home." They walked to his car. Before he had a chance to open the car door, Lynette was already back at the door of her house. He shouted, "I will be back tomorrow at ten if you will allow me. I really want to see you again."

"Okay," Lynette shouted. "Go now!"

After her soap opera was over, Lynette walked in the backyard, thinking, *Geez, he is a very touchy person, which drives me wild. I am glad Chester left when he did, for he was becoming hard to resist. As much as I desire sex in my life again, I do not want to jump between the sheets with the first man I meet. Why am I drawn to him this way? I have had several handymen of all ages but never have felt toward any of them as I feel toward Chester. My latest handyman, Pete, is in his midseventies and has accidently seen me nude coming out of the shower when I thought the front door was locked. Still, there was no desire to be intimate with him. Why should I become unglued when Chester merely touches me innocently with his hand anywhere on my body? Maybe it is because I have not sexually been with a male for over a dozen years, and I feel like a virgin all over again.* Lynette blushed and lowered her head as if someone had caught her doing something shameful, alone in her empty house.

Friday morning, Lynette ran from the car with the shell bag in her hand, stumbling on the soft, loose sand. A hand reached her arm, preventing her from falling. "Thanks," said Lynette. She looked at the person who was helping her. It was the beachcomber! "Hello, my knight in shining armor," she said. "Glad you were able to save me from falling on my face. Did you bring a bag today?"

"No! I was waiting for you. You are late! I almost gave up on you. I was going to go home. I already walked up and down the beach."

"I am glad you are still here!" Lynette wanted him to walk with her but knew he was a fast walker and did not like walking as slow as she did. Still, she teased him to walk with her and help fill her bag with shells. Lynette smiled when he reached over and took the bag from her hand. He said, "Come on, I will help you. It looks like rain with those dark clouds coming our way." As they walked collecting shells, Lynette thought, *We are very close, walking and bending with just a few inches away from each other, yet there are no intimate feelings for him like I felt when Chester was this near. Still, there is a comfortable feeling that I enjoy.* The sky became more threatening with dark clouds drifting faster to the shore; he grabbed her hand. "No more for today. We better make a run to the parking lot before it starts to rain," he said.

After putting the filled shell bag in the bucket in the trunk of her car, she saw he was leaving. Quickly, Lynette yelled, "Wait! You never asked, but my name is Lynette. What is yours?" He turned back toward her, grinning. "Why, Lynette, you gave me a name, Beachcomber! Don't tell me you forgot already? Today you called me your knight in shining armor. Of course, you could shorten that to just 'Knight.'" Lynette wondered, *Why won't he tell me his name?* In the midst of her thoughts, Lynette heard him say, "John

Johnson. Most of my friends call me J-J. You can decide what to call me. I will answer to any name you wish to use." Lynette asked, "How does 'Jay' sound? That is spelled J-A-Y. You will know it is me calling you." Nodding his head, J-J agreed. He added, "I can recognize your voice no matter what name you call me." They stood there staring at each other for what seemed forever to Lynette. Suddenly there was a heavy downpour of rain, forcing them to scramble to get in their cars.

Chapter 3

Lynette drove home trying to stay away from the trucks splashing water on the windshield. She parked her car close to the house, leaving the bucket of seashells near the garden hose on the side of the house. She ran in the house drenched to the skin from the rain. Lynette dropped her wet clothes on the floor as she ran into the bathroom to take a quick shower. Lynette was in a hurry to go to Eggs Your Way Restaurant where Gloria, her favorite waitress, would have Lynette's order ready at the time Lynette agreed to be there.

Lynette was greeted by the hostess. Lynette said, "I want my favorite seat, that booth in the corner. Is it taken?" The hostess took a quick peek while standing next to Lynette. Nodding her head, she said, "It is taken. Come, I will find you another seat to your liking." They walked to the middle aisle where Lynette was offered a booth facing the row of tables in front of the big windows showing the parking lot and those entering the establishment.

Lynette was disappointed and mentioned it. Before she sat down, a gentleman at the table directly in front of Lynette heard the conversation. "Come to my table. I don't like to eat by myself," said the man who looked like an elderly model. Not a hair on his head was out of place. Lynette sat down at her table, saying, "I do not know you." *Wow, he is the best-looking man I have seen since coming to Florida. He could be stepping off a page in a fashion magazine*, she thought. The man was now standing by her booth, offering his hand to Lynette. She shook his hand. "This is foolish!" she said. He announced, "My name is Quinton. I know you are not fond of where you are sitting because when you look straight out, you will be staring at me. I know how to fix that problem. How about sitting at my table? Don't worry I won't bite, and you can pay your own tab." She refused. He returned to his own table as they continued talking. Quinton stood up saying, "We can talk easier at one table and not disturb others. Should I move over to your booth?" Lynette was almost finished eating. She said, "Next time I come here and my special seat is taken, I promise you I will be your breakfast companion." No sooner did she say those words that Quinton seemed to shrink into his seat. A short, stout woman quickly walked past Lynette to Quinton's table, placing her large purse on the seat next to the chair as she sat down. She looked at Quinton, then at Lynette, with puzzlement in her eyes. Quinton said, "Had you come and sat at my table, you could have given my wife a bit of competition." Lynette winked at Quinton's wife, saying, "I don't like sitting alone, and your hubby is so handsome I wanted to join him, but he insisted he was waiting for his wife." Lynette hoped her lies were believed with no hurt feelings for his wife. On her way to the cashier, Lynette stopped at their table and said, "Let me introduce myself. My name is Lynette." The woman said, "My name is Katharine, with a *K*. Be glad you did not join Quinton as he never carries on a conversation. Quinton always has his head stuck in that newspaper." Lynette noticed the newspaper was still folded.

Gloria gave Lynette her bill and the wrapped, lopsided coffee cake. "I hope the coffee cake looks the way you want?" When Chester came, Lynette planned to have home-brewed coffee ready and this coffee cake, which she hoped he would think was homemade. Lynette was grateful for the extra courtesies that were always given to her by all the employees. "Yes, it will be perfect for what I have planned, "she said.

Chester arrived right on time. Lynette heard him enter the front porch with the slam of the screen door as she picked up the last of her wet clothing from the floor, dumping them in the hamper. When Lynette opened the door to the porch, she was almost out of breath. She wondered if Chester took this as her delight in seeing him again. Lynette whispered, "Glad to see the rain stopped. It was coming down so hard. Before, it looked as if someone held a garden hose on the front of my windshield with water gushing out." She was holding her throat as she spoke with only whispered words coming out. Finally, her voice came back in the right tone as Chester said, "Hush, you talk too much." He pulled her to his chest, giving Lynette a long and tight hug, while lightly kissing her lips. Lynette eagerly hugged his warm body, which she could feel though the white cotton T-shirt he wore. After several minutes, Lynette gently pushed Chester away. She said more calmly than she felt, "That is enough. You drive me wild. You were given the house tour yesterday. I planned on going out to the patio for our coffee, but everything is wet now. How about if we watch some TV and have our coffee and coffee cake in the living room?" Chester sniffed in the air. "Sounds okay to me, but I don't smell any coffee. Is it made?" Lynette giggled, "No! I have a jar of instant coffee. It is a mix of various Mexican blends, but the coffee cake will sweeten the bitterness away."

He is a good sport, Lynette thought. He drank all the coffee in the large mug to the last drop, and that was not Maxwell coffee. Last week, Billy, her son-in-law, had a small cup of that coffee and gagged on it. Still, she could not keep from laughing softly when she saw Chester take out a small pill bottle. He took one pill, swallowing it without water.

Lynette squealed, "You did not have to drink the coffee all up. I know it is very strong and bitter. My son-in-law, Billy, doesn't like it. I have gotten used to the taste. Next time, I will make real coffee, not instant." Chester merely blew his nose on a used, crumpled handkerchief that he pulled from his pants pocket. "It was okay," he said. Pointing at his scar on his chest, he said, "I had a heart attack a few years ago, and I cannot tolerate the indigestion pain. I sometimes take these pills before any side effects, to be on the safe side. Believe me, it was not your coffee."

Chester could not sit still. He kept walking around the room, which was a combination of kitchen and parlor. Lynette thought, *He acts like an animal on the prowl trying to catch his prey off guard.* When Lynette finished her coffee, Chester immediately took her empty cup to the sink, rinsing it off. In the meantime, Lynette settled down on the sofa with her legs dangling. She pulled the footstool close to the sofa, placing her legs on it, stretching her body out full-length. Lynette patted the sofa cushion next to her. "Come sit here. We can watch something on the TV."

It was an invitation Chester could not refuse. In an instant, he was not only sitting on the sofa next to her, but he also had his legs stretched out on the footstool. He lay on his side with his one leg on top of Lynette's legs. He was kissing her face gently while pulling her body tight to his chest. It felt so good she did not even try to stop him, but she returned his tender kisses with a hot longing kiss. He was practically on top of her; still, she did not stop Chester from feeling all of her body, until she felt his hardness poking at her thigh. Chester was holding her body close to him with his left arm on her shoulder, letting his other hand roam up and down her leg, stopping just below her short shorts, ready to slide his hand under her shorts.

"No! No more kisses. You better go home," Lynette said. Chester quickly moved away from her, jumping to his feet. He knew the word "no" meant to stop, or it might be considered an assault, possibly rape. "When can I see you again?" he asked. Lynette nervously said, "If you really want to, my daughter Ruth and Billy, Ruth's husband from Tampa, will be here next weekend. We usually have breakfast at Eggs Your Way Restaurant about nine or ten." Chester was now standing with his car door open. "Why not tomorrow?" he asked. Lynette thought, *I am getting those sexy stirrings in my groin. If he doesn't hurry up and go home, I may take him to my bedroom right now. What would he think of me if I did to him what I have imagined?* Lynette said, "My son, Sam, and his fiancée, Sue, will be here tomorrow. Are you sure you want to meet them? What if there are too many questions we may not know the answers to without a meeting of our minds?" He answered, "I can get around any questions he asks even if I have to evade them." Lynette said, "Okay! How does Sunday morning at eight for breakfast sound?" He nodded his head okay. Lynette wondered why anyone would want to be thrown in the midst of a lion's den, which would be easier than meeting her overprotective children, especially her son.

Chapter 4

Sam and Sue arrived late Saturday night with pizza, salad, and Samuel Adams beer, which they purchased at a convenience store where Sam filled his rented automobile with gas.

One of the first words Sam said after giving his mother a bear hug was, "I paid more for my gas here than in New Jersey and had to pump it myself." Lynette agreed. When she moved to Florida from New Jersey, she had to learn how to pump the gas into her car. Sue said, "I do not know how to pump gas. In New Jersey, it is still against the law to handle the gas pumps unless you work at the station." They ate and talked about all the news of the family, including their up-and-coming marriage, till after midnight. Finally, Sam suggested they go to bed, or no one would be getting up to go out for breakfast before noon. Lynette agreed. She wondered if it was too late to call Chester and change the time to later on. Lynette decided to call Chester, hoping he would not be mad at her for phoning at this late hour.

She was glad Chester's answer machine was on; Lynette left a message: "Time has changed to about nine or later. I will call you at seven about the time we will be going out for breakfast."

Sunday morning at seven, Lynette phoned Chester, "Could we go out to eat breakfast at ten or later?" she asked. Chester replied, "I had wakened up at six and heard your message that you would call me if breakfast was still on or not. I could not wait any longer for you to call, so I had cereal about six thirty this morning. I still want to meet your son. I could have pancakes about ten thirty or eleven."

Lynette suggested, "Why not just forget about going with us for breakfast? We can always go somewhere else another time." Chester was adamant about going to breakfast with them. After all, the seasonal tourist will be filling up the restaurant, and they would be lucky to eat before eleven or later with the long lines. Lynette hung up the phone wondering. *Why would Chester eat at home so early when he knew we were going to eat breakfast together?*

Breakfast was almost at noon. They had left the house at ten thirty and had to wait for their name to be called to have a table; Sam did not want a booth. It seemed as if there were not enough waitresses to go around, yet Lynette knew more waitresses were working this Sunday than during the week. Lynette had introduced everyone to each other while waiting for the table. Lynette looked Chester straight in the eye as she lied telling the story of how Chester was an old acquaintance who had returned to Florida for the winter season again this year. Anyone hearing Lynette explain about Chester's living situation would assume they knew each other a long time, not just a week. Lynette placed the toss-away camera on the tabletop, smiled, and said, "We are going to have a photo of this memory. Remind me to have the waitress take our photo when she has time."

Just then, a man stopped at the table, placing his hand on Lynette's shoulder. He asked, "Want me to take your picture?" Everyone stared at this man who was smiling at them. Lynette did a double take of the man. "Oh my goodness, Quinton. What are you doing here? I mean, I know you are here to eat, forgive me." Introductions were made, but Lynette did not elaborate upon how she met Quinton, just that they had bumped into each other the other morning. No one asked questions; Quinton took two photos of them, one from each side, to be seen from a different view. Gloria stopped at the table after Quinton left, saying, "I see Quinton found your table. I hope he was not annoying, Lynette. You remember how he gets sometime." Lynette blushed saying, "Quinton was no problem. He even took our picture."

Leaving the parking lot, Chester asked, "Lynette, when can I see you again?" Lynette wished Chester would just leave. She did not want to hear any more questions. She tilted her head saying, "My son and I have made plans. Why not call me on Tuesday evening after they leave?" Upon getting in the car, Sam asked, "Why didn't you ask Chester if he wanted to join us?" Lynette quickly answered, "Chester does not drive at night. I don't want him hanging around us all the time. He had been in this area a long time and surely has a lot of friends. He does not need us."

The next few mornings, Lynette walked the beach collecting seashells with Jay for an hour or so. Chester did not call Tuesday evening. Wednesday morning, he drove to Lynette's house. He pondered where Lynette could be. One thing for sure, she was not home; still, he did not move his car from the driveway. As he waited, he wondered who Quinton was. He had his nerve to stop at their table in the restaurant trying to talk with Lynette. Chester was happy there was no room at the table for Quinton to sit with them. As Chester looked up at the rearview mirror and saw Lynette's car coming in the driveway, all his thoughts about Quinton disappeared from his mind. Lynette drove her car past Chester's car into her garage, which she opened with the remote on the dash of her car. Chester walked following Lynette's car into the garage. He needed to be with her. All Chester could think about was taking her in his arms now. The last time he remembered having these feelings toward any woman was when he proposed to his wife years ago.

Once they were in the house, Chester held Lynette so tightly it took her breath away. She pushed him away. "No, I've got work to do. You have to go home. I don't want you to just drop over without phoning first." Chester, eager to please her, said, "Yes, ma'am!"

Lynette said, "Just go home now. I will be free on Friday. No, my daughter Ruth and Billy will be here sometime Friday till late Sunday. You can't come till after they leave."

Chester pleaded, "I want to meet them, and you have to admit I was good with your son, Sam. I believe Sam likes me. I know I enjoyed myself with Sam and Sue."

Lynette was silent for a minute or two, then finally agreed, "Let's make it Sunday." She thought, *Perhaps Ruth should meet Chester.* Then she would not have to worry in case he was here when Ruth or another family member was here. Lynette said, "Remember the same story I told Sam? That story will go for anyone we meet, even your family or friends."

Chester paused before leaving the garage and asked, "Are you going to phone me with the details, or should I call you on Saturday if you are not too busy?" He seemed nervous as if he was worried that she was giving him his walking papers. Lynette answered with a smile, "Same place, but this time let's plan to meet at the restaurant at ten o'clock. We will probably have to wait this time too. I will have Billy reserve our seats." Chester mumbled, "Maybe we should get together before Sunday." Lynette said, "Just be there if you want to please me." Chester insisted. He wanted to please her in any way she wanted. Lynette said, "Go home now, and I will see you Sunday."

They held hands as they walked to his car. Just before opening the car door, Chester put his right hand on his thigh near his crotch, gathering his shorts and squeezing. Lynette just stared at him. Chester said, "See what you do to me?" Lynette was amazed. "That is probably all clothes," she said, thinking no penis could be that size.

Chester still had his hand on his penis, saying, "Baby, this is the real thing. My cock is real hard. Put your hands here, feel for yourself how hard it is. Believe me, you cannot bend this tree." Lynette laughed to herself, thinking, *All men are almost the same size, yet there is talk about how important inches are. Chester looks as if he could fill my insides and make my blood start pumping.* Chester was getting more desirable by the second.

Lynette hurried back in the house and quickly sent an e-mail to Ruth about her feelings for Chester. These e-mails must stay between the two of them. She did not want Ruth to share what she wrote in this or any other e-mail about Chester with anyone, even Billy. Ruth sent a reply that every word would be kept a secret and asked to be kept informed in all that happens.

Lynette e-mailed another message; there were three tests for Chester to be a keeper. He has passed the first test by being confident, very easy to be with. The second test would be if he showed up at the restaurant on Sunday, keeping the story of her lies intact. "Yes," she murmured, "I will tell Chester that Ruth knows the truth of our meeting only a week or so ago."

Lynette received an e-mail from Ruth which read, "Mother, what is the third test for Chester to pass?"

Lynette e-mailed a reply to Ruth, "Sex has to be good!"

Chapter 5

When Sunday came, Lynette asked, "Billy, do you want to drive?"

"No! You drive. I will sit in the back. I know you and Ruth want to talk."

Lynette looked at her daughter and wondered if Ruth slipped and said something about Chester. Ruth noticed her mother look questioningly at her, and Ruth shook her head. When they reached the Eggs Your Way Restaurant parking lot, Ruth said, "Billy, quickly go reserve a table for four." Billy hollered, "You mean three, or do you want an extra chair for your mother's leg with the psoriasis? I thought she only has psoriasis on her fingers now." No one answered. Billy began to trot to the restaurant, passing the patrons waiting outside the building with "remotes" in their hands.

After Billy was no longer within hearing range of them, Ruth said, "Trust Billy to think of that."

Lynette saw Chester walking toward them. Chester stopped just past a group of people. Lynette wondered what he is waiting for. *Why doesn't he come to me? I know he sees us. Now he is making me nervous.* Lynette said, "Ruth, I need to use the bathroom. Come with me now before we are seated at the table." As they passed Billy near the entrance, Ruth pointed where they were headed and motioned for Billy to wait where he was. As they walked past the bench that Chester was sitting on, Ruth stared at him as he looked at Lynette inquisitively.

In the bathroom, Ruth said, "Geez, did you see that guy staring at you?"

"Ruth, that is Chester," said Lynette.

They returned to where Billy waited to be notified that their table was ready. Lynette and Ruth stood next to the nearest bench from the restaurant's entrance. There was no space left to sit on any of the benches. Billy was standing a few feet away talking to everyone and anyone who carried on a conversation with him. Lynette did not see Chester, but suddenly she felt a warm hand on her shoulder. It was Chester. When Lynette introduced Chester to Ruth and Billy, she told the same story to them as she had told to Sam. Lynette added, "Chester lives in Gary, Indiana, during the hot, humid summer months. He is renting a condo on Venice Island, within walking distance of Venice beach." Immediately, the remote in Billy's hand began to flash lights and vibrate. "That is us. Time to get our table," announced Billy.

Billy happily slapped Chester on his back while they walked to their table saying, "So you are a snowbird. How do you like Florida?"

"I am a sunbird, not a snowbird. I go where the warm sun shines. Florida has been my second home for many years," Chester replied with his arm around Lynette's waist.

Before sitting down, Ruth said, "We have traveled quite a lot. If I could afford to live anywhere, I would live in Colorado during Florida's humid summers."

"Everyone to their own poison, whether it be drink or where you live. I bought my condo as of Friday. I can now come and go all year long." Chester had his eyes on Lynette as he spoke about the condo. She wondered, *How come he never mentioned anything to me about his buying this condo.*

After eating, they sat drinking too many cups of coffee. No one wanted to leave the restaurant. Chester had his arm draped over the back of Lynette's chair, with his hand gently rubbing her shoulders and neck. She loved his warm, gentle touch and the rocking motion of Chester's leg against hers. She was glad they were sitting as her legs were turning to Jell-O.

Gloria, their waitress, stopped at their table explaining that in a few minutes she was going home to watch the big football game on TV. Lynette had already told Chester it was to be dutch treat. She would be paying for Ruth and Billy's breakfast because Ruth had fixed Lynette's computer. Lynette reached in her purse and gave Gloria her well-deserved tip so Gloria would not have to wait till tomorrow or for her paycheck to get her tip.

Soon after Gloria left their table, Chester asked, "Should I leave a tip, or was your tip enough for all of us?" Lynette knew Chester did not have much money, but she thought, *If he can't afford to leave a tip, he should not go to a restaurant. He should only go to a fast-food place. He could have said something before coming here. I am not paying for him in any way.* Lynette did not answer Chester. She only shrugged her shoulders. Chester put down one dollar. Billy wanted to see the big football game, which meant it was time to go home.

On the way home, Lynette said, "Don't tell a soul about Chester 'cause I am not sure what is going on yet." As soon as they walked into the house, Ruth mentioned she was not feeling well and was going to lie down on the bed in the guest room while Billy and Lynette watched the game. Lynette was not into sports and only watched the game to keep Billy company. Billy was full of questions about Chester, but he pretended to be interested in the game. He finally said, "I think Chester is a gentleman. I like him. He is a down-to-earth kind of guy. I can tell he likes you." Lynette changed the subject by asking questions about the game. Billy kept returning the conversation back to Chester. He asked, "Just what is the story with Chester? Are you two a couple? Should Ruth invite him to Thanksgiving dinner?"

Lynette replied, "No! We are not a couple, just acquaintances. Don't tell anyone about Chester. I don't know if he is a keeper yet. Don't ask me any more questions unless you want me to answer those questions with lies."

Monday morning, Lynette was up early, not being able to sleep; she did not feel like tossing and turning in her bed any longer. It was still too dark to go to the beach. All her chores were done. She drove her car to the beach and sat in it until it was light. She walked down the footpath to the beach, heart racing. Would she see Jay walking at a distance on the beach? Or was she too early? After all, it was only seven in the morning. She collected a bag of shells, keeping her eyes out for Jay; he never came. Disappointed, Lynette drove home with thoughts jumping around in her head. *Maybe I was too early. Maybe I should have stayed a little longer. After all, the shells could have been placed in the trunk, and I could have just walked on the beach, which is great exercise. Maybe next time I will do that.*

Lynette went to her favorite restaurant where Gloria teased her about just who the new man in Lynette's life was. Then Lynette went home, exercised on her patio gym equipment, tried to read the newspaper, and showered for the second time that morning while waiting for Chester to phone. He had told her he would call, but it was almost noon. She wondered if it would be okay if she called him. Lynette felt her pride leave her body as she dialed his number. She sucked in her breath, holding it for a second or two as she waited for Chester to answer the phone. Her heart skipped a beat when she heard Chester say, "Hello!"

Lynette said, "Hello, love. It is me! How would you like to come over to my house today?" She waited an eternity. She wondered if he had other plans, or maybe was just bored with her.

Chester said, "I can't today. I made previous plans. Lynette, I do very much want to see you. Tell me when you are available, and I will check my calendar." Lynette felt crushed; a tear fell from her eyes. Softly, she said, "How about coming here tomorrow and crawling back into bed with me, or did you make plans for the whole week?" She waited. the silence was deadly.

Chester said, "If I made any plans for tomorrow, I would break them because that is the best offer I have had in years. Just tell me what time?" Lynette whispered, "Around ten or so. Not earlier."

Chapter 6

Lynette was awake most of the night, drifting off to a deep sleep at four in the morning, so she slept in late. She cooled her burning eyes with the cold water she splashed on her face. *There is no time to go to the beach or even go out to eat breakfast,* she thought. She took a shower, letting the cold water spray on her face. She dressed into her baby-doll pajamas, sprayed her body and her bedsheets with White Shoulders perfume. Lynette never had much patience waiting for anyone, but it was still too early for Chester to come over. *Maybe I should read the newspaper,* she thought. *It might be relaxing while waiting for Chester.* She opened the living room door and slowly walked out toward the front-porch door. As she was about to pull open the porch door, it opened without her touching the doorknob. Lynette jumped back a few steps. With her mouth open, Lynette let out a startled scream until she realized the shadowed form was Chester. He caught her as she fell slightly into his arms against his chest. "There, there, it is only me," whispered Chester. Lynette was happy. She thought, *He is here!* He can't wait either. Lynette was nervous, yet no one would know. She reached out both arms pulling Chester close to her body. She took his hand leading him to her room, bringing him to her bed. She lay down between the sheets without removing her short silk pajamas. Chester climbed onto the bed with all his clothes on except his shoes. Lying on top of the quilt, he gave Lynette a hug and immediately lay on his back.

Lynette whispered, "Take off your clothes. I want to feel skin against skin." Chester jumped up off the bed, quickly pulling his polo shirt over his head and dropping it to the floor. He loosened his belt and swiftly took off his shorts and underwear together while Lynette stared at his body, trying to see his coveted penis. The way he had bent his body, she could not see his penis. Staring at his body, trying to get a peek, she lifted the top sheet.

"Hurry, get under the sheet. It is cold," she said. Without another word, he climbed under the sheet and took Lynette into his arms. She whispered, "Did you remember to lock the front door? I would not want my handyman, Pete, to just saunter in to the house."

Chester ran to the door. In a flash, he was back, sliding in between the sheets, pulling Lynette into his comforting arms. He wiggled the rest of his body against Lynette's now-naked body.

"Woo! You are cold!" Lynette said.

"I will warm up quickly next to you," he said huskily.

"Oh, damn!"

"What! What's the matter now?" he annoyingly asked.

Without thinking or blushing, Lynette whispered, "I want you so bad I can feel the moisture between my legs."

"Lynette, that is good! You have to be wet, or it won't go in. I brought some KY Warming Jelly, which we will not need now." He gently rubbed his hands all over her body. Lifting the top sheet off her body, he said, "It is time to explore your beauty." He slowly kissed her throat, sucked on her nipples one at a time while rubbing the other with his thumb. Moisture was building more and more in her private area. She wanted to go to the bathroom to wipe her vagina dry; yet she lay there while he continued to kiss her body, going lower and lower. Chester raised his head saying, "Don't shave anymore, I enjoy seeing a pussy with hair." Grabbing her crotch, he said, "That is why this is called a pussycat."

Lynette calmly said, "I never was a hairy person. As I grew older, the chemo medication I took for my psoriasis caused me to lose what little hair I did have. My companion, Tony, told me many times that he enjoyed kissing me down there without the fear of a strand of hair getting caught in his mouth. Chester, I am lucky to have hair on my head!"

Chester teased, "I guess I should call you Baldy Cat!" Lynette playfully punched him on the chest. "You better not if you know what is good for you." Lynette let her hands slowly massage his body and feel his penis; it was limp. *Where had all that hardness gone?* she wondered. "Chester, we talked too much. Your penis shrank. What can I do to help you get an erection again? I really need you."

"No, Baldy Cat, it was nothing you or I did. As much as I want you too, the big fellow will go limp until it gets used to you, my sweet Baldy Cat."

"Chester, do not call me that name unless you want to be called Fizzle Out," said Lynette, annoyed.

He was quiet for a moment, just lying on his back. He turned on his side facing Lynette, resting his forehead on his hand with his elbow against the pillow. With his other hand, he let his fingers draw the outlines of her cheeks and nose. Lynette started to speak, but Chester gently rubbed her lips with his thumb, which tickled Lynette, and he stopped. He cleared his throat and whispered, "Do you remember when you saw the scar on my chest the first day we met? I told you I would explain another time how I got the scar. A few years ago, I suffered a heart attack—not a warning but a full-fledged attack. I will never forget. I was at a restaurant when I started to choke. Then after coughing, I still had trouble breathing. I had this crushing pain. It was as if someone was standing on my chest. I couldn't breathe out. It was bursting my lungs. At the same restaurant, two paramedics were having lunch. I was rushed by ambulance to the hospital emergency room. Within minutes, the hospital staff rushed me to the operating room. I was lucky the best surgeon was still at the hospital and able to give me a heart bypass, or I would have died."

"Oh, my love, how awful. I thought it was from the Korean War. Are you comfortable having sex?"

"Yes, Baldy Cat."

Lynette put her hands up playfully in a fist toward him but did not touch him.

"Okay, Lynette, I was only teasing. I won't do it anymore. Give me your hand." She placed her hand in his palm. He placed her hand on his penis, showing her how to slowly rub it up and down and then squeeze his penis. Taking her hand away from his penis, she climbed on top of him, kissing him all over his bare hairless body.

He placed his hand on her head, running his fingers through the top of her hair gently. Lynette was now kissing his body lower and lower as he gently nudged her head lower to his crotch, holding her head there.

"Kiss my cock, baby. Run your tongue up and down the shaft. Yeah, that's right. Now with your tongue, lick my cock as if it was an ice cream cone that is dripping along the sides from the sun. Now really suck harder. Yeah, that's it! Oh, baby, please don't stop," he moaned as he moved his hips up and down.

Lynette tried to do as she was told. However, she was only able to lick the head of his penis. Otherwise, she felt as if she would puke. *Oh my god,* she thought. *He just squirted in my mouth.* She spit it out on to her hands and his penis. As Chester started to pull her up to face him, she wiped her mouth with the sheet. She heard him say, "Sweetheart, you are a tiger. The best sex I have had in years. I think I told you I have not had any sex since my heart bypass operation. Thanks for the loving."

Lynette stared at him thinking, *He is now satisfied, but what about me. I still have a need to be filled inside.*

Lynette whispered, "If this was the first time you tried to fuck since your operation, were you afraid you might die? Was that the reason why you lost your hard-on?" Chester lightly kissed her nose, saying, "No. It was not the fear of dying. Not that I want to die, but I didn't have a willing partner till now."

Lynette cuddled up to Chester, putting her leg on top of his leg. "You do know you are the first man I have been involved with since Tony? Well, you're really not my first man yet. I wanted you so bad that I was dripping with sexual desire. Did I turn you off somehow? I know you were hard, but when you tried to push it in, the damn prick turned into a soft rubber toy. Maybe I am too old for sex because that was not how I remember it should be."

Chester held her in his arms. "Let's just cuddle for now. We have to give it time. We need to practice more just like newlyweds. Lynette, next time it will be your turn. I promise you."

Lynette had to admit she liked to lie in his arms while he talked of his life growing up on a farm, joining the navy, his marriage, his divorce, his daughter, his heart attack, his thoughts and dreams before he met her. He told her more about his finances; he had enough money if he was careful. Not that he was poor, but with the new increase of the house taxes and house insurance, it had put a strain on what and how he spent his money. She snuggled a little closer to Chester's body; he gently lowered his lips to hers giving her a quick kiss while he spoke. Lynette thought, *I won't add to his money problems. We can always go dutch on any plans we may make. Still, I wished the act of making love had worked.*

"What are you thinking, Lynette? I can almost see the wheels going around in your head."

"I wonder if it will ever be good with me being so moist. I wonder if it will slip out, or if you do manage to get your cock hard enough to stay in, will you feel anything with me being so wet and slippery," whispered Lynette. He was quiet. She added, "When the newness of our bodies wears off, maybe I won't be so moist. I want to be only moist enough for your penis to go in, but dry enough so we feel something."

Chester kept quiet while still hugging Lynette, wishing she would leave the matter alone. Didn't she realize how he felt about not being able to complete the act of making love? "Hush! You talk too much. Just snuggle next to me for a few minutes. I am trying to get it soft. It's in a semihard condition. Maybe we can screw in a few more minutes. What you did was very good, and I enjoyed that. Don't push."

When Lynette saw the sheet move off his groin area, she placed her hand on his penis. Lynette sat up and looked at Chester's body, including his penis, and was shocked to see such a small prick. *Holy cow, my son had a longer penis as a toddler,* she thought. "What size are you? Have you ever measured your penis?" "Yeah, when I was a teenager, I did and found out I am average. The big fellow is six inches. Like I said before, I am average in height, weight, and down there." Lynette thought, *He has just lied to me. No way could his cock ever be more than four inches, just a little longer than my middle finger. Maybe he could buy those extenders I heard about on the late-night TV commercials. If our sex does not improve, maybe I can order some for him. For now, it is pleasant resting my shoulder on his strong arm.*

They lay on the bed a few more minutes, but so quietly that Lynette almost fell asleep. He, on the other hand, got restless and jumped up, pushing Lynette out of his arms. "My arm is falling asleep and becoming numb. Let's get up and go somewhere to eat."

"I guess it is time to get up and take a shower." She ran naked into the bathroom, quickly showering. She came out of the shower and saw Chester standing in the bathroom doorway just as in her fantasy dream. "Did you take a shower, or were you waiting to use this one?"

"I am dressed. I don't need to shower, I took one before coming here," said Chester. Lynette was now brushing her teeth. She glanced in to the mirror with her mouth full of toothpaste foam and saw Chester's reflection in the mirror staring at her. She asked, "Are you going to stand there and watch me?" Chester shook his head, smiling. "Yeah."

She felt funny putting her partial false teeth in her mouth with him staring at her. "I took them out because I did not want to bite you."

"Next time, bite me!"

Lynette was now putting on her clean clothes. "Are you really going to watch me get dressed?"

"Yep," he said.

Lynette wanted to put on her makeup without Chester staring at her. She asked, "Why don't you use the other bathroom to take a shower. You can put on something from Billy's closet."

"I am not taking a shower."

"You will smell like sex if you don't take a shower."

Chester lowered his head, sniffed the air close to his body. "I like the smell of sex."

Lynette gave Chester a quick kiss on his cheek. "You better go out to eat by yourself. I just remembered I have to go to the cleaners and have to get to the bank before it closes."

Chester gave Lynette a big grin. He knew she was upset because he refused to take a shower. Well, he was planning to go to the Dome where his buddies hung out. He wanted to take her there to have a late lunch, hoping at least one of his friends would see them. Later he could brag to his other buddies about Lynette. He wanted his friends to know he just had sex with a female who could not get enough of him. He knew they would be jealous. How many times did he tell them to use it or lose it? A few of them hadn't had an erection in many years. He knew, for they had moaned to him about it. Lynette was annoyed but was trying hard not show it. She heard him say, "When can I see you again?"

"Friday will be okay if it is good with you?" Chester nodded. Lynette shook her head, "No, that is no good. I won't be home till late. I am going to Tampa to spend Thanksgiving Day with Ruth and Billy. What are your plans?" Lynette prayed he had plans and would not be alone for the holiday, but there was no way she intended to bring him to her daughter's house with all the family just waiting to devour him with all kinds of questions.

"You do not have to worry about me. My daughter is having a big turkey meal and all the trimmings. Today during lunch, I was going to ask if you wanted to come with me to my daughter's house. I have spoken so much about you to my daughter. She wants to meet you. I am sorry you have other plans."

Lynette was looking in the mirror at her reflection. She swallowed; her throat was dry. "I will call you when I get home on Friday, or you can call me sometime on Saturday when you get a chance." No sooner were those words out of her mouth when she heard the front-porch door slam shut. *Did I hurt his feelings?* Lynette wondered.

Chapter 7

Lynette returned to her home Saturday, around two in the afternoon, from Tampa, driving way over the speed limit because she was excited. Her heart was beating hard as she dropped her overnight bag to the floor; she was in a hurry to check the answering machine. Deep in her heart, Lynette knew there might be several calls from Chester. Lynette wished she had given him her cell phone number. She thought, *He is probably home anxiously waiting for me to call to let him know I am safely home.* Lynette listened to the answering machine tape a few times, repeating the various messages; none was from Chester. Lynette stayed indoors, carrying the cordless phone to whatever room she went in to; tears kept filling her eyes, causing her nose to be runny. She kept sniffing, feeling all alone in the world.

Sunday morning, Lynette went to the beach hoping to see Jay. She did not realize how much she had come to look forward to walking on the beach with Jay; however, Jay was nowhere to be seen. Lynette felt suddenly very lonely watching the couples sitting or walking on the beach. Lynette wanted to talk with Belinda about Jay and Chester. She stopped collecting shells and ran to her car. "I will call her as soon as I get home," she said out loud to no one.

At home, she tried to call Belinda, but she was not home. Lynette could not even leave a message on the answering machine; it was not working. Lynette threw caution to the wind; she dialed Chester's number. "Please be home," she prayed. His answering machine tape was waiting for her message at the sound of the beep. "I could use your help tonight or tomorrow with decorating my tree—that is, if you want to help me with the decorating, or who knows what else we might do. Give me a call. I will order pizza."

She lay in her bed wondering if Belinda was alone on Thanksgiving. *Did Belinda have to work, or was she with her new friend Erick? Belinda had explained that Erick wanted to get physical, but Belinda felt it was too early.* They had been sneaking kisses at work. They had been seeing each other for three months, still in the smooching stage like teenyboppers. Yet Belinda had confided that she was finding it difficult keeping her hands off him. Belinda was having a hard time keeping Erick's hands from roaming when they were hugging. *What would Belinda think if she knew I had gone to bed with Chester? The act was not as satisfactory as I thought it would be, but should I tell Belinda that?* Lynette heard the phone ring. It was Belinda. "Lynette, sweetie, can you take me to my mechanic's place on Route 41?"

Lynette was not doing anything else and needed this distraction. "Sure. What is the problem? Wait, it is Sunday. Don't tell me the place is open!"

Belinda explained she was having trouble starting her car at times. She needed to drop her car off there for the night. Lynette offered to drive Belinda to work in the morning, but she was told that Erick would bring her to work and take her to the mechanics after work. Belinda was giggling. Lynette felt a tinge of jealousy. Lynette wanted the kind of feelings that Belinda and Erick were having.

Lynette asked, "After we drop off your car, can you help me put up my Christmas tree? We can make a party of it. I can pick up some pizza and your favorite beer, Coors Light." Belinda didn't want to disappoint Lynette and agreed to help a few hours with the decorating. "We can talk about men, sex, and what comes out of our mouths with too much drinking,"

They had pulled all the boxes with Christmas decorations and the big artificial Christmas tree into the house from the big shed. Together they struggled on the front porch making the tree stand straight. Belinda was opening the boxes, looking for the strings of lights; Lynette was in the kitchen with the beer and pizza. "Come on, Belinda, let's go out on the patio and start our party. Bring the paper plates."

Together eating pizza and drinking a few cans of beer, conversation was flowing easily. "Well, Belinda, how about bringing me up-to-date on you and Erick. You guys must be up to something because you are never home like you used to be. I can remember when I tried to get you to go out to have coffee at the Dome Building, which is only a few streets away from your house. Your excuse for not going was you were too exhausted from work. Now you are taking walks around your neighborhood or just going for a drive to one of the fast-food joints. You are never home, and I miss you."

"Okay, I did not tell you, but Friday night he gave me a single red rose when I was leaving to go home from work. You know we both had to work Thanksgiving Day, and the best part of the day was that we worked the same shift. Lynette, I was touched by Erick giving me the rose, which he kept hidden from everyone all day. Well, I got the nerve to ask him if he could go with me to the beach Saturday evening to watch the sun set."

Lynette interrupted, "What did he say? Doesn't he have to work Saturday night?"

"Erick agreed to meet me at the pavilion on the beach. He would ask Ray, a coworker, to stay the extra few hours for him. Erick will pay Ray out of his own pocket if he needs to. I was at the beach waiting for him with a bottle of champagne and a blanket. But there was a problem at work that only Erick could take care of. I almost went home. Lynette, I felt as if someone had put a knife to my heart. I am in love with Erick. I did not think that would happen.

Lynette thought, *Last year when Charles, the roofer, had asked me to go out, it was Belinda who pointed out how the only thing I knew about Charles was he put up my roof. Now here she is, dating a coworker whom she really knows nothing about. Yet I do want her to find someone to spend the rest of her life with. Still, what about me? I don't know what I am doing or even want.*

"Lynette, you were right about Erick and me. I am glad I took your advice."

"Tell me, Belinda, what happened? Was he able to go to the beach?"

"Yeah, he came, and we were walking on the beach almost all by ourselves. The sun had set over an hour before, and it was getting dark. Suddenly it started to rain, and I do not mean just a sprinkle. We ran back to the pavilion to get some cover to protect us. Erick wanted us to go home so I would not get sick, but I surprised him. I suggested we go sit in my car, which was closer to us, and wait for the rain to slow down. I gave him the bottle of champagne to open, and we got warm under the blanket. We laughed so much as we drank the champagne from the bottle. I forgot the glasses at home." Belinda stopped talking; she put her finger to her lips and motioned with a nod of her head toward the patio cage door. No one even breathed. They heard the back door to the house close and then the scuffing sounds of footsteps. All at once, the cage door swung open, and they saw a man's silhouette standing a few yards away from them. Both women screamed, hugging each other.

"You left your front door unlocked again," said a man's voice.

"God, Chester! You scared the hell out us," screamed Lynette.

"Sorry." He walked over to the women, pulling a folding chair toward him. Lynette introduced them quickly with no explanation of who they were. Chester said, "I came over because you left a message on my answering machine, but I see you have the tree up. I don't think you are able to put the trimmings on the tree tonight, so don't even try. In your condition, you might fall and hurt yourself."

"Chester, help yourself to a beer, or if you want, there is hard liquor and wine in the office cooler," said Lynette. "We finished off the pizza," she added, giggling. Belinda was quiet looking from one to the other as they spoke. Chester stood up. "I don't drink or attend any party that is nothing but a drinking party. I used to be an alcoholic when I was younger. I do not wish to spoil your party. Just be careful you do not fall in the pool. I will call you tomorrow about helping you to decorate the tree. Nice to have met you, Belinda. I am sure we will be seeing each other again. Don't bother walking me out. Stay where you are. I will lock the front door behind me."

Lynette thought, *Why did he bother to come? He did not have to be so mean. He spoiled our mood.* Truly, the mood of the party had changed. It was not over, only just beginning again. Belinda asked, "Is he your new man?" Lynette meekly whispered, "We met in October. My son, Sam, met him before Thanksgiving. Ruth and Billy have also met him, but I have not told anyone else about him."

Belinda interrupted, "You never told me anything about him. You have known him since October, which is almost two months now. What is going on?"

"It is because I do not know what I feel, let alone think, about him. It is not like you and Erick slowly doing your thing. I took him to bed, and now it is so confusing. I don't really want to be seen out with him because when he goes back home to Indiana, I may be asked too many questions that I have no answers for."

"Are you telling me you have been having sex?"

"We went to bed just before Thanksgiving Day. It was absolutely the best sex I ever had." "Lynette, if it was that good, he must have been having sex when he was up north. You better be careful. He may have a disease like

AIDS or something else. Lynette, please. Whatever you do, don't give him any money even if he says he will pay you back."

"Belinda, is that the only reason you think Chester has sex with me?" asked Lynette.

Belinda felt she was put on the spot because she knew how easily Lynette could be persuaded to be generous. Belinda tried to change the subject, "Erick and I had sex last night in my house. It was late when we left the beach. Erick followed my car home. He wanted to be sure I got in the house safe. I made us coffee, and we sat side by side on the couch without drinking the coffee until I could no longer hold my head up. I suggested he stay in the guest room for the night. The next thing I knew, we were having sex. We stayed the rest of the night in the guest room bed, which left us getting hardly any sleep with our naked bodies touching all night. However, sex with Erick was a lot of fumbling, almost as if we were virgins. Erick must not be as knowledgeable about sex as Chester. You are lucky that you are both sexually compatible. Please, Lynette, don't repeat what I said about sex. I do need him. I do not want to live alone. I will do whatever it takes to keep Erick interested in me. I love him!"

Lynette wondered, *Why did I lie to Belinda that sex with Chester was so good. It is the pits. Unless he does something different, I may just drop him from my life.* Lynette hugged Belinda. "Give it the time the two of you need adjusting to each other in that department. You have all the other bases covered. The best part is you both need and love each other. I don't know yet of my feelings or, for that matter, Chester's." It was getting late, and Belinda had to get up early Monday morning. Lynette suggested leaving everything just as it was for her to put away later that night or tomorrow.

As Belinda was getting into Lynette's car, she said, "Lynette, it is so good to have girl talk. To be able to really say what is on each other's mind without the other getting hurt feelings. Let's always be this way." Belinda had her cigarettes out of her purse, then remembered Lynette's rule about no smoking in her house or car, so she put them in her jacket pocket.

Chapter 8

A few hours later, Lynette heard someone at the door. *Who could that be?* wondered Lynette. She jumped up out of her bed and grabbed her robe. As she walked to the door, her heart was pounding. *Could this be Chester? If it is, I will take him back to bed with me. Oh, just the thought gives me the desire to make love. I must stop being a romantic!* It was not Chester but Lynette's handyman, Pete. Lynette felt so let down.

"What are you going to do, sleep all day?" asked Pete. Lynette looked at the big clock hanging on the front porch wall just beside the screen door. "For crying out loud, Pete, it is only ten in the morning. I admit I was asleep. I thought it was the middle of the night."

"I am here now. Is there anything you need to have done? I have a few big jobs that I have to do for a real estate company, which might last past Christmas."

"Do you want to help me finish decorating the tree?"

"Nope, I am going home. I will be back to see how it looks later on. Maybe tonight. Say, just where is that fellow with the Indiana license plates who is hanging around? He should be helping you do odd jobs instead of me. Lynette, don't get involved with any man who can't be bothered to do a few small chores around your house."

"You are my handyman. He is my lover!" They were both laughing as Chester's car pulled up the driveway. Pete whispered, "Watch me get rid of him." Pete opened the front-porch door. "Hey, pal, you are just in time to help with the decorating of Lynette's Christmas tree." Lynette watched Chester squirm. Chester said, "I came to let you know I won't be able to help you with the Christmas decorations. I promised my daughter I would help set up her fresh Christmas tree. I will call you when I am done. Maybe we can have coffee."

Lynette answered, "Okay." She thought to herself, *He can't help me, but look at him run when his daughter has a chore that she needs a man's help with. Well, so far, Chester is not turning out to be the keeping kind of man I thought he might be.*

Late in the afternoon, Lynette was finally finished with the Christmas decorations on the front porch. However, something did not look right with the tree. Maybe it was her imagination, but the tree looked as if it was leaning. Lynette poured herself a glass of wine, walked to the front porch, and sipped the wine as she stared at her completed project. She was thinking how she did not need anyone to help her with any of this year's decoration. Lynette always had Ruth or Billy take the responsibility in previous years for the Christmas tree and window decorations. They even decorated the outside of the house with strings of lights. This year she would be doing all the decorations by herself; of course, there would be no stringing of lights on the house. Lynette had put up the artificial big Christmas tree with Belinda's help last night; now it was beautiful with the lights lit up. Suddenly, Lynette realized, the tree not only looked as if it was leaning, but it was also indeed falling. She needed instant help. Lynette dialed Pete's telephone number on her cell phone.

Pete's wife answered the phone, recognizing Lynette's voice, and yelled, "Peter, pick up the phone! That woman from Maple Brook Road is on the line. She sounds as if she is in trouble!"

"What is it you want, Lynette," asked Pete.

"Come quickly. My tree is falling over. I am holding it up as I speak!" Pete was annoyed with her. He had told Lynette he was busy with an overload of work. Lynette was now begging, "Please Pete, I need you as I never needed anyone before. This tree is standing up only because it is resting on my back."

Pete was rushed out of his house by his wife. Pete only lived a street away from Lynette; he has stopped by her house before turning in to his street many times. However, he felt she was being a pest right now. This could have waited till morning, and he was tired.

He opened Lynette's outside porch door. After seeing Lynette almost to her knees with the Christmas tree lying on top of her back, Pete took over the situation. He lifted the tree up off her back, pushing Lynette out of the way. He did not realize his hand and shoulder were pressing on her breast, until Lynette gave a yelp, "Ouch!"

"Get out from there. Can't you see I am trying to straighten this tree?" He looked where his hand was and, smiling, told Lynette to have the empty bins ready because a lot of the ornaments were coming off the tree. Lynette grabbed a nearby clothes basket, quickly placing in the ornaments that Pete handed to her from the tree. Pete used the thin wire he brought from his house and fastened up the wire in a triangle design. "This tree is not going anywhere now. You better call me when you are taking it down."

"I hate seeing that wire. I know it has to be there, but look how ugly it looks." "Lynette, hand me those Christmas cards from the table." Pete hung on the back wire a few of the cards. Lynette was not happy. "It does not look

Christmassy." Pete took the tinsel trimmings from the window and wrapped the tinsel around the wire over and over, covering the wire; then he hooked the Christmas cards on the wire. "How does that look, mademoiselle?" Lynette threw her arms around his neck. "You are the greatest! How much do I owe you?" she asked. Pete said, "Wait, I have something for you from my wife." He took from his jacket pocket a few twigs of mistletoe, holding them over Lynette's head. Pete kissed her, which Chester saw as he walked in the opened door to the front porch.

Chester was wondering what the hell was going on with Lynette and her handyman but kept quiet.

Lynette asked again, "Pete, how much do I owe you?"

Pete grinned. "No charge. That was payment enough. Just give me a call if you need anything, day or night."

Chester walked in to the living room with Lynette, waiting for her to explain, but she didn't say a word about why Pete was always here. Chester was trying to be patient as he remembered several of the times he had seen Pete leaving Lynette's house, and how gullible he was to swallow Lynette's explanation of Pete being only a handyman. Surely no one could have that many chores twice in one day. It didn't make sense. He also wondered what Pete's wife's thoughts were about her husband hanging around there so much and not being paid.

Lynette offered coffee, but Chester refused it. "Lynette, I only came here tonight thinking maybe we could, you know, maybe talk. But it is late, and I better go home. When can I see you again?"

Lynette's mind was going fast around in circles. "Before you go home, how about helping me bring in that skinny artificial old Christmas tree from the big shed? I had planned on tossing the tree out this year, but I have so many ornaments left over that Pete took off the big Christmas tree." She was thinking of what Pete had said earlier about how Chester should want to help her. *Bringing in the other Christmas tree is a small request. I really don't need anyone to help me. Belinda and I were going to set up both trees last night by ourselves. However, our plans changed somehow, and it got late.*

Chester gave Lynette a hug, and kissing her, he whispered, "Want to go to bed and see what flames we can start? You know you set off sparks in me whenever you are in my arms. Remember, I told you it was your turn this time?"

Lynette shook her head. "No, I need a shower. I want to get that tree in the house and, maybe, trim the tree before going to bed tonight."

Chester turned, started to walk away from Lynette. He heard her say, "Want to hang the mistletoe before you go so you can kiss me next time under it?" Chester sternly said, "I don't need a mistletoe to get a kiss, only a willing partner." He blew her a kiss and was gone. Lynette stood there going over what he said or what she thought he said.

A couple of tears fell from her eyes as she dragged in the old Christmas tree from the shed into the house, feeling sorry for herself. Lynette did not need or want to struggle with this old scratchy tree, but it was now the principle of it all to prove she did not need anyone. One thing was for sure, if Pete's wife ever dumped him, she knew there would be a fight from all Pete's female customers to keep Pete for themselves. It was late, but Lynette stayed up till both trees were brightly shining with all their glory. The windows were stripped of the decorations, but they no longer needed any, with the old decorated tree standing in front of the window.

Chapter 9

Four days had passed without seeing either Jay or Chester. Lynette was lonely. She had not even heard from Belinda. It was December 1, which meant Lynette had to fix the timer for the Christmas tree lights to go on and off at a special time. She was struggling with the tiny arrows on the timer. The front door opened without noise, and Belinda came up to Lynette, holding some mistletoe in her hand. "Merry Christmas, Lynette. This is my gift to you."

Lynette told Belinda about Chester and Pete and how she had turned Chester away, knowing he was interested in having sex but not helping her like Pete said he should.

Belinda said, "Good for you! You are not getting any younger. Not that you look your age, but you know. I do not think Chester is the right guy for you. Maybe Erick has a friend. And, for goodness sake, think first before you act. Remember Chester will be going back to Indiana in a few months. Don't let him use you."

Lynette wanted to really confide in Belinda as she had with Ruth. Lynette had told Ruth that her sex life with Chester was lacking something, almost to the point of her not wanting to do it at all. Ruth only advised her mother to do what she wanted and no more.

Belinda pulled a travel brochure out of her purse, a travel brochure showing various cruise destinations. "What are you doing with those? Are you planning to go somewhere soon?" Lynette asked curiously. Her thoughts were now of jealousy. *Everyone but me has a wonderful life with someone to share it with. Maybe I should call Chester and invite him over tomorrow.* Belinda, waving the brochures, said, "Erick can't afford to go, and neither can I. I wish you and I could go somewhere someday, but I am broke. Someone left these brochures at the nursing home where I work. Look at the bargains that are for five destinations. It would be like getting a present from the big guy."

Lynette asked, "Who is he?"

"Who is he?" repeated Belinda as she began laughing and continued until tears ran down her cheek; she finally found the words, "Why, Santa Claus. You know, the guy who puts gifts under your tree."

Lynette quickly said, "Thanks. However, I am not going to use them either, but I want to show them to Chester to see what he says. Maybe he will offer to take a trip with me someday. Wait, these brochures are good only till January, so we can't go. Belinda, I have a busy week. I need to prepare for the family Christmas party on December 8. I am picking up Joyce and her hubby from the Sarasota airport on the seventh. You do know you and Erick are expected to be here for my party?"

Belinda was not sure if she could get Erick to go to a party where he does not know anyone. Lynette explained, "Roy, Joyce's husband, and other men from the family will be here." Lynette wondered, *Maybe I should ask Chester if he would like to come.*

Belinda had to go home. As she was leaving the front porch, she asked, "Are you inviting Chester to the party?" Lynette bit her lip. "I am thinking about it, but I haven't decided." Belinda hugged Lynette. "I know I can get Erick to come if I told him you had a new man in your life and needed him to be here to help keep Chester entertained comfortably without the family ganging up on him with questions."

"I am not sure if I want to expose my involvement with Chester just yet to the family. It will all depend on what Chester says," said Lynette. The phone was ringing. Lynette gave a quick hug to Belinda.

Lynette wondered, *Why am I running? There is an answering machine.* Still, Lynette ran to the phone. "Hello!" she said.

"This is Chester. Is it too late to come over tonight?" Lynette answered quickly, "Anytime you want to come over is never too late. Do you want to spend the night?"

"We will see. Tonight is your turn to be satisfied," said Chester. Lynette hurried into the bathroom and hunted for the shower cap. She was able to shower and put on her long red silk nightgown. Lynette finished spraying herself and the bedsheets with White Shoulders perfume when she heard Chester open the door. Lynette had left the Bose Radio on the Dove radio station that played the oldies, and now Jim Reeves was singing, "Put your sweet lips a little closer to the phone, and let's pretend, my darling, we're all alone." Lynette put her arms around Chester's neck, standing close to him, and started to sway her body to the music. She wanted him to dance with her; instead, he brushed her away from him. "Let's go in the bedroom." He took her arm and lightly pulled her with him.

Chester slowly backed her to the bed; Lynette did not get on the bed fast enough for him. So he reached over and scooped her up in his arms. He then laid Lynette on top of the quilt on her king-size bed. Lynette looked up at Chester thinking, *How strong he is to have picked me up like I was a rag doll instead of 165 pounds.*

Chester said, "You won't need this," as he raised her nightgown up over her head and tossed the gown on the floor. Lynette now had nothing on.

He bent over Lynette, smoothed her hair with his hands. Within seconds, he was on her bed lying on his side letting his hands roam all over her body. He reached up over her head, pulling a pillow from the top of the bed, and placed it under Lynette's lower back and hips, which lifted her pelvis upward to him. Lynette did not know what he was trying to do but was eager to just let Chester do whatever he had in mind. After all, it was her turn. Lynette noticed Chester had not removed his clothes, but did not mention it. She did not want to break the mood she was in.

He was now kissing her belly, then moved his face, kissing her right thigh; he brushed his lips across her vagina as he moved his head to the other thigh, which he then was giving wet kisses. He held her breast lightly; Lynette breathes a deep sigh and opened her legs as wide as she could with his heavy body on top of her. She waited for Chester to kiss her anywhere between her legs and was about to ask him to when he started to lick and suck her clitoris, driving her to high peaks of sexual desire. Lynette lowered her head. She wanted to see his face while he made love to her. Their eyes met as he was looking at her to see the reactions on her face. Lynette could no longer control her emotions. She moaned over and over while pushing his face deeper in her vagina and holding his head between her legs to keep him there until she finished climaxing. Lynette was finally drained and took her hand away from his head. She thought, *I just adore what he just did. He is a keeper after all.*

Chester now had put her legs up over his arms. Lynette wondered, *Now what is he trying to do? Oh, he never took off his clothes and is trying to get his penis out of his pants.* Within seconds, he pushed his penis into her body. She could feel the movements but was in a position where she could not move. He was slamming his hard cock in to her vagina; she could feel it filling her insides with its throbbing. *How did his penis grow so big?* she wondered. When it was over, they both ended up on their sides exhausted.

Chester said, "What a workout! I told you one day it would be your turn. I know you enjoyed it. I gave you all I had and then some." Lynette hugged him. Dreamily, she said, "Oh, Chester. That was the best sex I ever had. You are a keeper. Let's get dressed and go out to eat, your choice."

Chester put his penis back inside his pants. Lynette, giggling, said, "Chester, you never took off your clothes. You didn't wash your penis. Aren't you supposed to wash it every time after sex?"

"I am going home. I will take a shower then. You take your shower and get some rest."

"I can make you a sandwich or a steak if you want? You can stay overnight here with me. We don't have to go out anywhere. It is late."

"Lynette, I can't stay, I must go home now. Tomorrow, my daughter, Jenny, has made plans for us to go to the Strawberry Festival at Plant City. I do not want to disappoint her. I will call you later this week."

"I am having a Christmas tree party on Saturday, the eighth. Do you want to come and help me move the furniture around, maybe on Monday night?"

"You go about your plans on the big meal you are having for your family. You mentioned you were picking up your daughter Joyce and her husband from the Sarasota airport Friday. Maybe I can see you on Wednesday or Thursday." Lynette was disappointed. *Maybe he didn't understand I want him to be here to open gifts with us. I will wait till I see him again before I let Chester know how much I want him at my party.*

Lynette went to bed with a magazine since she did not feel sleepy. The phone rang. Lynette dropped the magazine as she reached for the phone. "Hello."

"This is Chester. I didn't wake you, did I?"

Lynette was hanging almost off her bed, trying to retrieve the fallen magazine. She was pressing her chest against the bottom of the mattress, and her voice was shaky as she asked, "Chester, is something wrong? Did something happen? Are you all right?"

"Lynette, you talk too much. You never give me a chance to say anything. Nothing is the matter! I only called because I thought maybe you might want to come with Jenny and me tomorrow to the Strawberry Festival." A loud thump was heard as Lynette fell off the bed. "What was that sound? Are you okay?"

"Yeah, I was getting the magazine that fell from the bed, and I slid off the bed landing on the floor. I am not hurt. Well, maybe slightly bruised."

Chester cleared his throat. He again asked Lynette if she wanted to join him and his daughter tomorrow. Before he finished, Lynette said, "I would love to tag along, but I can't. I have things I must do for the Christmas party." They talked for a few minutes, but in a strained way as if each one had something on their mind but was not expressing it in words.

Monday, Lynette moved the furniture around till there was enough room to have a long table to fit fifteen adults and a small table for the three children. Name tags were placed at each plate. Lynette used the rest of the day to shop for food and other supplies for the party. She was tired but still started to get all the equipment needed to cook and set out the spices. She decided to make four pounds of meatballs and freeze them. She had roasted the turkey while moving the furniture and decided to slice the turkey and put in the freezer. Saturday morning at five, she would put the frozen food in the Crock-Pots with various gravies and sauces.

Lynette did not go to bed till about three thirty Tuesday morning. She tossed and turned until she put the bedroom TV on, watching the old movies. Hearing a bang at the front porch, Lynette got out of bed. Taking her cell phone, she went to search out where the noise came from. Lynette was relieved to see the newspaper lying in front of the screen door. That was the noise she heard; all of a sudden, she was very sleepy.

Chapter 10

Later around nine in the morning, Lynette awakened and felt someone in her bed. She knew this was silly but sat up and looked over at the other side of the bed that should be empty. There was someone lying there looking at her. She was startled, and her eyes could not adjust to reality. Perhaps she was still asleep and dreaming. A hand reached out to her and touched her arm. Lynette screamed!

Chester moved closer to Lynette, holding her shaking body. "How did you get in my bed," asked Lynette.

"I knocked on the door, and it opened. I thought you left the door slightly ajar for me. I let you know I was here. I kissed you and heard you say come to bed, so I did," explained Chester.

"I was sleeping. I worked late last night and did not fall asleep until after five this morning." Lynette was now in Chester's arms. She noticed he had no clothes on. She continued quizzing Chester, "Why didn't you phone or something? Why would you just walk into my house, my bedroom?" Tears stung her eyes; she felt as if she was being imposed upon. Surely, Chester was taking a lot for granted.

Chester was annoyed. "Do you always leave your door open for anyone to enter?"

"I opened the door for the paper. Maybe I didn't close it tight enough, and the vibrations from the traffic on the road pushed the door ajar. I was too sleepy to be sure, but I thought I not only closed the screened door but also locked it," said Lynette. She was now getting aroused and started to cuddle with Chester. He wanted her to give him oral sex, and she obliged. She rolled off him, wiping her lips with the sheet. It was wet with her spit.

Chester tried to push his penis in her but could not do it. Lynette pleaded, "Give it to me. I need you inside now." But Chester slid his body up off her; he lay on his side, pulling Lynette into his arms. Lynette was moving her bare body all over his upper leg. It reminded Lynette of a male dog trying to dry hump a human's leg. She stopped moving. "Why didn't you put it in?"

"I couldn't. It was too soft. You were too fast for me. Next time we will need less foreplay," said Chester. Lynette thought *He wanted me to suck him. Why is he trying to put the blame on me?*

Chester got up from the bed. He did not look at Lynette as he dressed; he heard her mumble something but not the words. He said, "My comfort zone is gone. I need to get some air. Get dressed, I will make coffee. We can drink it outside in the backyard."

Lynette scrambled out of bed, headed to the bathroom. She grabbed her clothes from the floor on the way. Her feelings were hurt. She was taken too long on spite until she heard Chester knock on the bathroom door. "Why did you lock the door? I wanted to wash your back," he hollered.

Lynette opened the bathroom door and gave Chester a hug, which he returned tighter. "Forget the coffee. I have to go to my friend Belinda's house," she lied. "What time is it?" Before he could answer, the phone rang; it was Belinda. She needed help with her car again. The conversation that Chester heard was, "I am so sorry I am late. I know I was supposed to be there before ten. I will be there in a few minutes."

He hung around a few more minutes, cleaning the countertop and rinsing the cups and coffeepot. Chester thought this was one female he was never going to understand or satisfy. Why try?

Lynette met Belinda at the mechanics garage on Route 41 across the highway from Wal-Mart. Belinda jumped in to Lynette's car, saying, "I am hungry. Let's eat at McDonald's in Wal-Mart?"

"Sounds good to me. Do you want to shop first or eat first?"

"I wrote out a list. With your help, we can be finished in a jiff. You are not your jolly self. Did something happen, or don't you feel well?"

Lynette slowly answered, "Chester came over this morning and didn't phone first. You called at the precise moment I needed to send him on his way, before an argument was started." Belinda kept silent, so many questions she wanted to ask. However, knowing Lynette, questions only made Lynette say what she thought you wanted to hear. They hurried loading the shopping cart with the items on her list. Soon Belinda was pushing the cart of groceries to the parking area for carts near the McDonald's eating area. Lynette did not buy a single item of groceries; her excuse was she was on a diet. Belinda started to look for another place to park the cart when a clerk placed a tall basket with pastries on clearance in front of Belinda. "Just make sure we can see the cart when we eat," said Lynette. Lynette got in line and started to order for the both of them when Belinda came up and stood beside her. Lynette said, "Go find a table for us where we can see the shopping cart and talk without being too close to other people. I will pay for this. You can pay next time."

"Oh, Lynette, you shouldn't have to pay. You are doing me the favor," said Belinda. Tears came to Lynette's eyes; she sniffed and shook her head with her eyes looking at the floor.

The eating area was crowded, and in spite of Belinda's effort to park the cart where it could be seen from their table, the view of the shopping cart was blocked by a few customers standing in front of them. Seeing the tears almost falling down Lynette's cheek, Belinda was too curious to be quiet any longer. "Did I hurt your feelings? It is not like you to be so depressed. Can you talk about it to me?"

Lynette sniffed a couple more times and swallowed. She explained, "This was the same table Chester and I sat at the first day they met." To gain her composure, Lynette guzzled her coffee, which had become room temperature. Belinda offered to get a refill for them; when Lynette started to put up a fuss, Belinda mentioned it was free. That put a smile on Lynette's face, and she said, "What the heck, go get it. I am quite thirsty."

Belinda was refilling their paper cups for the third time with coffee when a male customer standing next to her waiting for his turn at the coffee urn was fidgeting. Belinda, without looking, said, "I am sorry, I know I am taking too long. I can't get these lids on the cups."

"Do you need any help?" he asked. Hearing his voice, Belinda turned and looked at his face. "Hello, Chester! Fancy we meet again and so soon," said Belinda.

Chester made believe he did not recognize her. She said, "I am Belinda, Lynette's friend. She is over at that table." He looked where Belinda pointed. Chester already knew Lynette was at the table, for he had followed her car from her house trying to stay a few cars behind so she did not suspect it was him; he even lost her for a moment. Once in the department store, he almost bumped into her a few times; he finally waited in the men's bathroom several minutes. He had thought she might have seen him and had been giving him the slip, but no. He saw her through the entrance of the open golden arches. He had planned on pretending to be surprised at seeing Lynette. Now here was Belinda taking him to Lynette's table where he could sit without an invitation from Lynette.

"Hey! Look who I found," said Belinda. Lynette looked up and smiled. "It is good to see you for the second time today. Do you have time to stop by my house later on? You left so quickly this morning that I did not have a chance to show you something that you may find interesting." Lynette was quickly rambling without really giving Chester time to speak. When she finally paused, her face was beet red, and she smiled hearing Chester say, "What time, Lynette?" Feeling her composure had returned, she answered, "Well, I must take Belinda home. She lives on Oak Lane at the end of Maple Brook. But we have to get in line to pay for her stuff in the shopping cart."

Belinda interrupted, "That will probably take forever. It seems roots grow on your feet at the checkout line." Chester said, "Scat! I will clean the table. I will wait for you in your driveway. I don't have a key. Ha-ha!"

The girls loaded the trunk of the car. Belinda whispered, "Don't look now, but Chester is sitting in his car at the back of our car."

Lynette thought, *He will probably follow us home*, which he did; but he did not turn off onto Oak Lane. He continued to drive up to Maple Brook Road into Lynette's driveway and waited for Lynette to come home.

So he thought, *She wants to use my joy stick as her private lollipop. Imagine, twice in one day, which is okay with me.* She made him feel glad to be a man, and he did not care if she was satisfied. As long as she wanted to lift him up to heaven, so be it. He felt a warming in his groin just thinking about Lynette.

He heard her car's tires squeal as she turned sharp in her driveway, almost missing the driveway; for a second, he thought her car was going into the gutter. He lost his erection, leaving a slight dampness in his briefs. He followed her into the garage. They walked silently into the kitchen; all the while, he stayed a few steps at the back of her. He wondered why she never offered him a hug or kiss, just walking hurriedly in front of him without a backward glance.

He reached his arms out to her in the kitchen, but she did not allow him to kiss her by stepping back away from him. *Now what is on her mind*, he wondered. He did not say a word, only let her lead the way.

Suddenly she turned to him and, giving him a peck on his cheek, looked into his eyes with a curious smile on her face. He didn't want to but slowly felt his own face loosen the tightness in his brow; she still wanted his body.

Lynette held his hand, slightly pulling him toward her bedroom. She stopped next to the long table that was set and covered with a couple of sheets, waving her arm out over the table saying, "Check this out. Help me remove the sheets." He did. He saw over a dozen name tags, one at each plate setting.

He could not stop himself from walking around the table, picking up every name tag, reading each name. Where was his? he wondered. He cleared his throat. "Lynette, this is a lovely dinner party setting. Did anyone ever tell you that you are a great little hostess?"

Lynette was now hanging on to Chester's arm saying, "These are mostly Ruth's family and, of course, Belinda and Erick. I am missing only one more setting. Guess who I would like to be here at this Christmas dinner party?"

Chester knew she meant for him to beg her, but she could never find the time to meet his daughter, why should he join her family? He said, "I am glad you were wise enough not to squeeze a setting for me."

"Chester, would you like to join my table? You can sit next to me."

"There is no room for me anywhere, anyway."

Lynette said, "That can be solved easily. This is not one long table but a few folding tables. I have a couple of small folding tables that I can put here at the end where you and I can sit across from each other." She walked to the end of the tables, trying to show him how it is no trouble to make room for him to join her party.

Chester put his hands on her shoulders. "It is too early in our relationship for me to be meeting most of your family, but I thank you for offering me an invitation." He hugged her and put his thigh in between her legs, wiggling against her private area. He pushed his thigh upward and felt her tremble; he lowered his hands from her shoulders to her ass and pulled her body tight to his.

"Oh god," she moaned. With her mouth open, she closed her eyes; she felt weak, almost drained. She knew if he didn't hold her so tight she would slip down to the floor into a melting puddle.

Lynette took Chester to the guest bedroom. "My bed is not made."

Chester was slowly walking behind her, nibbling on the back of her neck, blowing in and around her ears, knowing she was getting weak in her knees wanting him. Yes, he had her aroused, and if he was not fast enough, she would slide along his body to the floor—possibly unzipping his shorts—and, on her knees, suck his joystick dry. He wondered what that would feel like as he tried to keep her in one spot without losing his erection.

"It is okay to use your bed," he heard himself say. "We are only going to mess it up again." He tried to push her against the table, but she stopped him. Lynette said, "Be careful, or we will cause the table to fall, and who knows what will break. We don't have time for anything but making love in a clean bed."

Chester looked forlorn at her, wondering why she was wasting precious time. "You talk too much," he said.

"Wait, I have to take a shower and spray on some perfume."

Chester whispered, "Forget the shower and your perfume. I find it a bit too heavy and sweet smelling. I really prefer the scent of a woman's vagina. No smell in the world can come close to the scent of lust."

"I do not want to have any body odor. I want to smell nice for you when we make love."

Chester carried her to the bed in the guest room, dropping her on the bed. He quickly crawled into the bed without any clothes on; he sat up, removing the bed linens halfway off his body, showing his penis sticking straight out with a drip at the end. "Do I have to remove your clothes, baby, or are you going to tease me, removing one piece at a time as you wiggle your ass?"

"Do you want me to do the hula or striptease dance for you," she asked.

"Not now! Just give my joystick a few rough licks or even chew it. It is your lollipop, a regular all-day sucker just for you." He didn't care anymore if she had clothes on or not. He pulled her to his body, pushing her head down on to his penis. He knew he was being rough, but she was asking for it the way she was leading him on and teasing. He knew she wanted him to force her to do what she wanted, and then pretended to want something different.

There was nothing else to do but satisfy him first, and he would later make it her turn as he did once or twice before. It was easier for a woman to make love a long time, but men had only a few minutes or lose the erection and his desires.

"Next time we are going to do a sixty-nine act of love so you can control your emotions a little longer."

"Chester, just what is a sixty-nine? I have heard of that but always was a bit too shy to ask anyone." He heard her words but did not register what she was saying. Chester held her close to his body with her head almost in his armpit. He was sweating; he wondered if he had any strong odor. Now that their act of sex was finished, he noticed she had a body odor. He had earlier placed his two fingers in her vagina, and without her noticing, he put his hand to his nose and waved his fingers and slightly inhaled a heavy odor. Next time he would wait for her to use her perfume. He never heard of a man's groin area smell, at least not fishy like a woman. Yet her nose is now too close to his armpit. Heck, he heard many times that women loved the smell of a man's sweaty body, it turned them on. He wondered what was it that she said a few minutes ago about being shy; not this, baby. Whose mind was she trying to play with? Not his. He knew, regardless how innocent she pretended to be, it was only an act. He was not born yesterday and knew a wild, sexy tigress from a frigid iceberg.

His comfort zone was fading fast; he did not want to lie in bed any longer. Chester jumped out of bed. He dressed next to the bed while she stayed in bed under the sheets watching him.

Lynette whispered, "Well, have you decided to come to my dinner party?" She had her fingers crossed, hoping he would change his mind. After all, she knew he loved her sexual ways. Maybe he would want to spend the night one of these days.

All Chester said was, "You better take a shower and fix these beds. Remember your daughter Joyce and her husband will be here soon."

Lynette thought he did not have to remind her; after all, she was picking them up from the airport Friday, but today was only Tuesday. Well, if he didn't want to be here, maybe it is for the best.

Chapter 11

Around ten thirty Thursday night, Chester drove past Lynette's house on his way home from his daughter's. He had earlier gone to the drugstore leaving a prescription for the scrotal patch. The druggist had convinced him to use the "almost anywhere" patch. These are sex patches to help as a testosterone replacement. He used to buy the scrotal patch that could only be placed on scrotal or bony areas, but now he could wear this patch anywhere but on the scrotal. The pharmacist would have to call his doctor to change his prescription to this new patch that goes under the name of Androdrem, which he was told had to be ordered from the warehouse. Darn, he had just removed his last prescription patch from his scrotal after leaving Lynette's house yesterday at four. He remembered Lynette's fingers touching the patch, but she was so hyped up with him sexually she didn't ask him about it; probably she did not know it was there. He was tired and was going to have to space out these sex visits a few days, before he dropped dead from exertion.

He was edgy all night, thinking about Lynette, and he cut short his visit with Jenny when she kept steering the conversation to questions about Lynette. How could he say when the three of them would meet? No, he was not ashamed of Lynette or what they were doing. He thought about what Lynette had said about too many questions that she didn't know the answers to; well, neither did he.

All Chester knew was that he had to be on Lynette's street now, not to see her, but just to drive by her house.

He slowed down a block before her house. He could not believe his eyes. *What was Pete's truck doing leaving her driveway at this time of the night?* He drove hurriedly past her house and around the block a couple of times. He saw there was a light on in the house. He wondered if he should ring her doorbell; after all, it was late. What excuse could he give her? He wondered what kind of mood she was in. However, Chester knew Lynette was awake, for he saw with his own eyes Pete leaving her house, maybe her bed. The only thing that Chester knew for sure was he had to see her now, this minute.

Chester tried to open the outside screened porch door, but it was locked, which left him puzzled as it was never locked. This screen door opened to the porch, and as far as Chester knew, it didn't have a lock of any kind. He looked for a doorbell. He saw a metal knocker, which he used. He waited a few more seconds and knocked louder and banged on the screen door. He thought she had to hear him. *Why isn't she opening this door?* He worried that if he made too much noise, then the neighbors might call the police; maybe he should go back to his car and wait a few minutes till she made some movement like turning her bedroom light off.

Suddenly Chester heard movement; then he saw Lynette. She was wearing her flimsy nightshirt, and he wondered if she wore any panties under it. Chester felt his body getting aroused. Lynette didn't realize the hold she had on him, never asking anything of Chester but to have him perform the act of sex with her.

Lynette now opened the outside screened porch door, saying, "Well, look what the cat dragged in! I heard a noise. I thought it might be Pete. He just put a lock on the inside of the porch screen door. Still, I was not sure if I should check it out. Tell me what on earth are you doing here at this hour of the night?"

He did not wait for her to finish talking; he pushed past her, grabbing her arm and pulling her in to the parlor. They stood facing each other with no space between them. "I thought maybe now was the best time for learning the sex act of sixty-nine." Chester had his arms around Lynette, forcing their bodies into one; she could feel the pressure of his penis pointing between her thighs against her vagina. *Yes*, she thought, *this is as good a time as ever. I hope he doesn't wimp out.*

He pulled off her nightshirt; she was in her birthday suit. He almost ejaculated at that moment; Chester needed those patches this second to give him the lasting power. Damn, he did not want to have those blue ball pains again.

Lynette slowly walked him to the couch where he pushed her down easily and knelt over her body. He said, "See your clitoris is a button. Maybe I should nickname you button," as he played with her clitoris with his thumb, rubbing back and forth gently and in circles. "I will play with your button till you can't stand it and beg me to fuck you."

Lynette was getting hot and bothered with just the sexy chatter and his touch. She reached over, started to lick the shaft of his penis with long strokes of her tongue as he had taught her. Within minutes, he had twisted her body so they were side by side, and suddenly he was upside down sucking her so-called button. He was moving his penis in and almost out of her mouth, which she didn't realize as her thoughts were only on what he had emotionally stirred in her nerves till she was quivering with delight.

"Now," she begged. "Put it in, all the way in!"

"It won't go in. I shot my load."

"What do I do now? I am not finished!" Lynette felt his penis. "You are still hard. Why can't you make it go in?"

"Roll over on me." He moved with her body; now he was flat on his back with her body on top of his. "Sit up on me. You can try and push my penis inside of you. Squeeze your knees to my body and ride me. Yeah, that's the way. I can feel you. Baby, you are in charge. Do what you want. I can't move." Lynette slowly moved up and down all the way, "Oooh. Aaah! Ouuu! Mmmmmh," she moaned, now making soft high-pitched sounds like a kitten meowing, with her groin connecting to his groin as she moved. Her shoulders and head thrown back in ecstasy, they were one, and she was in control.

Finally, she collapsed on his chest, all sweaty and not caring if she smelled one way or the other; she was exhausted and completely satisfied. Chester rolled her off him and on to her side. He kissed her on her lips, noticing she still had not wiped her face of where he had ejaculated. He held her face with both of his hands; right this moment, she had the prettiest face he ever saw. He felt himself melt toward her, not in an aroused feeling but from his heart. He thought, *So this is love.*

Lynette asked Chester, "Why did you stop your part of the act of sixty-nine while I kept doing my part?"

"A woman can look up longer than a man can look down. You were really something, and don't even try to tell me you were not satisfied. Yeah, we made the clouds move, and you rode me to heaven."

They lay on the couch a few more minutes. Chester almost pushed her off the couch as he raised his body up and over her. He blew in her ear and whispered, "I loved your sexy sounds like a kitten meowing. Maybe I should call you kitten instead of buttons."

Lynette started to protest. Chester put his two fingers on her lips, saying, "Hush. It is okay. As much as I love a good fuck and doing most of the work, you can do whatever turns you on with my body, whether it be sucking my rod or riding me to heaven." He moved, and Lynette slid off the couch on to the floor. Chester made coffee while she quickly showered; while she rinsed her mouth, she heard the porch door close. *Darn*, she thought, *he is gone without so much as a thank-you for the loving.*

She heard the bathroom door squeak as it slowly opened. Lynette looked in the mirror, saw Chester looking at her with a cup of coffee in his hands. "I thought you left. I heard the door close outside."

"I went to the car for some donuts, thought you may need some energy after that."

They sat at the end of the table, trying not to spill anything on the prepared table as they drank their coffee, and quickly ate the dunked donuts. She knew this was not diet food, but she felt beautiful and slim. Chester stared at her, smiling fondly, waiting to hear how great their sex was; he just knew there could not be any complaints even without the patch.

"I am glad you did not leave before. Chester, are you sure you do not want to be at my dinner? We only eat, talk, and exchange gifts." She prayed he would change his mind and say yes.

"Enjoy your family. It is too early to explain that we are lovers. Here, this is for you. Merry Christmas," he said as he gave her a large wrapped gift.

Lynette jumped up and ran to the kitchen cabinet, bringing back to the table a small Styrofoam box, which she handed to Chester. "Merry Christmas from one lover to another. Please open it now!" Chester was all thumbs as he turned the box over and over. Finally, he pulled off the cellophane tape, separated the box in half. There was a black mug in the box. "Thanks, this mug matches the rest of my mugs. Counting this mug, I now have at least ten, and they are all black," said Chester, disappointed. *Why does everyone always give him a cup?*

Lynette said, "Wait, rinse it off with hot water and pour hot water or coffee in the mug." She almost dragged him to the sink, taking the cup from him, letting hot water run off. Then, in the cup, within seconds, a photo of them appeared on the outside of the cup. "Well, what do you think?"

Chester felt his eyes fill up with moisture; he was truly moved, and only she could have thought to make his gift a lasting memory. "I will cherish this gift and think of you whenever I drink from it. I love it," he whispered softly as he was all choked up.

They were now walking toward the door. Suddenly Lynette remembered she had not opened his gift to her. "Wait! I did not open your gift to me. Should I wait for my Christmas party to open it?"

Chester blushed. "Open it now, and please, whatever you do, don't show it to anyone." He watched her expressions on her face as she ripped open the wrapped gift.

Lynette wondered if it was a sexy nightgown that made Chester blush and hoped it was not candy. Finally, the gift box was unwrapped, and the box top was removed; inside was a red plastic pillow with a slip of paper with instructions. She did not read the words but looked at the pictures of different positions of a couple of people in the act of intercourse. "I don't understand," she said with puzzlement on her face.

"I could not seem to go deep enough for you—before tonight, that is. This is called a sex cushion. It is made for people our age. The pillow will fit your body and raise your pelvis to the right degree for me to enter without hurting you but giving you a thrill you deserve."

Lynette turned the cushioned red pillow over and over. "I never saw or heard of such a pillow. We will have to try it out one of these days."

They were standing next to the couch. He sat down and pulled her on to his lap. "I didn't give you the right gift. I am sorry, but this will set our sex on a level you will not believe."

Lynette was still confused but glad to have this special sex helper and thought, *My god, even he does not always enjoy our sex, which must be why he mostly wants me to suck him instead of fucking—*

He broke into her thoughts saying, "I love you."

She said, "Please don't say that unless you mean it." He began kissing all over her face. "Let me stay tonight, it is late. You never know what may happen later on, and we have to try out your gift," he whispered.

Lynette wanted this to happen for so long; even sex has started to begin to be as good as she remembered it should be like. The sound of an alarm was heard.

"What on earth was that sound? Did you set the alarm clock for a reason?" he asked.

"Yes, it is time you left. I got to get ready to go to the airport and pick up my daughter Joyce and her husband, Roy."

Chester started to stutter, "I . . . I forgot . . . I . . . I mean I knew . . . but I . . . Okay, I will go now."

Lynette was pleased with herself. Looking smugly, she said, "Chester, my love, I must start getting ready to go now. It is over an hour away to the airport. Their plane is arriving at four, that's only a few hours from now. Another time you can stay over, and we can snuggle all night long—since we have discovered how to make sex sizzle—but go now."

Chapter 12

Chester drove down the driveway thinking about how later that day he would go to the Dome where his buddies would be drinking coffee and how he would place his new photo gift mug on the counter for the waitress to fill with coffee, but for now, it was time for sleep in his own bed. He reviewed the night and almost felt a tug at his heart. What was he thinking about spending the night at Lynette's house? He did not want to be that involved.

Chester knew it would soon be time to leave Florida and Lynette. If he did not rent out his condo, he could fly down to Florida and see his friends and Lynette whenever he wanted to. Soon it would be time to say good-bye to everyone when it warmed up in Indiana. He loved to be there in the late spring till early summer, certainly not staying in Florida's hot, humid summers. He must watch himself with mixing up his sex acts with the feelings of love. He didn't want to give her any ideas of him staying all night. A woman can get nasty when they seek revenge for being dropped. So, regardless of how adorable she may be at times, he was not going to let himself get caught into her clutches like a fish on a hook. And he has no inclination of supporting a woman now or ever. There were plenty of women out there who were as sex hungry, in search of a man to satisfy their urges, as Lynette. She does not realize how lucky she is to be with him. However, for the time being, Lynette will do as long as she knew he was leaving her in June or July. He would keep in touch so he would have a warm body upon his return in the late fall.

Chapter 13

Lynette thought about how sex had changed from being good once or twice to now being great. It may be time to see what else they could do together that they would enjoy. *Who knows? Chester may decide to live in Florida all year. After all, we can always drive to Indiana anytime during the year since we are both retired. He can sell the house in Indiana and rent out his condo on Venice Island while he moves in with me. He will then have enough money to pay half of the bills, which is only fair. I don't want to pay for anyone, no matter how great sex is.*

All thoughts escaped from Lynette as she saw Joyce and Roy walk toward her; they were each pulling luggage on wheels. They stopped several yards away from her. Joyce pointed at the hallway, which had a sign with the word "restrooms." "I have to go to the ladies' room," said Joyce.

Roy continued walking to Lynette, but now pulling both sets of luggage. Roy gave Lynette a peck on her cheek. "Have you eaten anything yet?"

"No."

"Let's eat at the airport restaurant."

"It doesn't open till around seven," replied Lynette.

"What doesn't open till seven?" asked Joyce as she hugged and kissed her mother.

Lynette quickly answered, "Roy wanted to eat here, but I was telling him it is too early for the airport restaurant to be opened. But there are vending machines and tables over there." Lynette was pointing to the darkened area on the other side of the second floor from where they were standing.

Roy looked from one to another, raising his eyebrows up and down in a playful fashion, and slowly, he hunched his shoulders, bending over the luggage. "Lead the way. Just remember I am still asleep and starved." Joyce tenderly touched Roy on his cheek with her fingers.

"You are so sweet, Roy. Let's wait. In a few minutes, we will be by your favorite restaurant near Mother's house, the Cracker Barrow."

They were waiting for the elevator to come to the second floor, but the door did not open. Joyce kept pushing the button. A stranger mentioned there was probably someone getting on the elevator from the first floor; and maybe, they should wait a minute. Joyce crinkled her nose and smiled at the stranger. Suddenly she heard the whine of the elevator rising to the second floor. A few people walked out of the elevator, pushing and pulling several suitcases. The stranger gave Joyce a knowing look and walked away.

During the quick ride down to the first floor, Joyce said, "Mother, Roy's fishing pole could not fit in the upper storage but was being placed with the other luggage coming from the plane on to the carousel conveyor belt. Roy will go ahead and pick it up from there. We can sit on the waiting bench just next to the elevator."

Within minutes, Roy was waving his arms wildly at Joyce for her to come to him. "I don't know what his problem is, but I have to see what he wants. I will be right back. Stay here with our luggage." Lynette watched them talk and saw both of them going to the information booth. Joyce pointed for Roy to return to the conveyor belt of the luggage going around. She came back by her mother, laughing. "He has bats in his belfry. Would you believe Roy thinks he hears someone call his name over the loudspeaker? I heard nothing!"

Lynette thought she heard a name but could not understand who was being called; it was muffed with that high-pitched noise. *These people should have that fixed. I don't know how anyone understood that message.*

Joyce interrupted her mother's thoughts, "He is waving to me again. This man is driving me crazy."

In a few minutes, they were walking back toward Lynette, shouting and waving their arms around in the air. Lynette asked, "What is the matter?"

Roy loudly said, "They lost my good fishing pole. It was my name being called over the microphone. Our plane had taken off from Newark, New Jersey, and left with my fishing pole on the cargo area. So now there is confusion all around about my missing fishing pole."

Lynette said, "Let's leave my phone number and address at the information booth, and when it is found, we can then decide what to do."

Joyce was shaking her head. "Mother, the airlines found another plane that is flying to this airport, and then they will forward the fishing pole to your house. But Roy will not be able to fish today, and that was one of the reasons he came here to Florida with me on this trip instead of just coming here during the Christmas week."

Silently, the three of them walked to the parked car. Luggage was put in the trunk. When Lynette paid the toll leaving the airport, she looked in the backseat at Roy, who was drifting off to sleep. There was no need to look at Joyce who was already snoring loudly. Lynette quickly drove straight to Perkins Restaurant close to her house. She had chosen that restaurant over Eggs Your Way Restaurant because the coffeepot was placed on the table, and she wanted her coffee without waiting.

Chapter 14

For whatever reason, no matter the amount of coffee they all drank, once they were home, exhaustion set in and was relieved by going to bed till late in the afternoon; and even then, they were tired. Lynette realized there were no phone calls or messages from the airport about Roy's fishing pole. While she explained this to Joyce in the kitchen in a low voice, Roy still heard every word in reference to his fishing pole and became irritated all over.

Joyce was on the phone for over an hour, trying to get satisfaction. *Where is the fishing pole at this moment?* No one could tell her. As soon as the pole arrived at the airport, Joyce will be notified. She tried to tell Roy the same thing she was told; after all, it was in a plane, and no one can do anything but wait till the plane arrived.

"What is taking them so long to get here? I ate, went to sleep, and still not a word about where my fishing pole is. I think it is lost. I never should have allowed them to put it in another area. I should have stayed right beside the fishing pole all the time," Roy said in a high-pitched tone.

Lynette knew he was trying hard to get his composure back. "Roy, it is just an old fishing pole. If anything happens to it, the airline will replace it. Calm down."

Joyce agreed with Roy that he had every reason to be mad, and when she got back to New Jersey, some heads were going to roll. She paused a few seconds and then started to laugh. Roy could not find anything funny with what she had said. He was going to take a walk outside in the backyard.

Joyce was left to unpack the entire luggage, putting clothes in the guest room's dresser drawers and closet. *Why do we always bring so much and almost always wear the same clothes, which Mother always washes every night?* she wondered. The sound of the phone brought her to reality. Without waiting for her mother to answer the phone, Joyce grabbed it. It was the information clerk from the airport; the plane arrived, and the fishing pole was there. Lynette heard loud shouting, "No, we are not driving an hour to the airport and another one back home, not counting the sitting around waiting for someone to fetch the pole. Your company lost it and can just drive to my mother's house." There was silence. Soon Lynette heard, "I am not waiting here another minute. We are going out to eat, just leave the pole on the front porch." Silence again. Joyce was now explaining in a softer voice, "The porch is completely screened in with a screen door. It will be safe." She paused. "Thank you. I know it is not your fault, but look at it from my husband's point of view. He came to Florida to fish, and we are too busy tomorrow and are returning home Sunday. He has not been able to relax, worrying about his favorite fishing pole."

Lynette made supper at home, not wanting to go out and miss the cab driver. Roy was taking a shower in the guest bathroom, and Joyce was taking a shower in the master bathroom. Lynette was making sure all the linens and bedding was ready for anyone that wanted to spend the night. Ruth's family usually returned the same night on the day they arrived.

Finally, the dishes were put away, and the TV remote was in Roy's hands, which took his mind off the missing fishing pole. Later Roy and Joyce turned in for the night.

Lynette walked out to the front porch door, planning on locking up for the night. There in front of her eyes stood Roy's fishing pole without a bag, tackle box, or tags. She decided to wait till tomorrow to say anything about the pole's arrival.

Saturday at five in the morning, there was a lot of frenzy while Roy annoyed the women with his fishing pole story. Roy kept saying it was like Christmas finding the pole in front of the kitchen table.

Lynette had placed it there before going to bed the night before while Joyce and Roy were sleeping.

Around noon, all the guest had arrived and begun to hear of Roy's fishing pole's travel story.

Lynette knew every word of the story and could tell by Roy's voice that he would remember this trip longer than any other visit to Florida.

Billy wanted to read something in the sports section of the paper. He yelled, "Where is the newspaper?"

Lynette said, "It should be near the end of the driveway."

Roy and Billy walked out to find the tossed newspaper if someone walking past the driveway didn't pick it up and take it home. Within seconds of the front door being slammed, sounds of shouting male voices were heard in the house coming from outside.

Joyce and Ruth almost bumped into each other racing toward the door. Soon they were all laughing, leaving Lynette to wonder. Did they catch someone walking past her driveway picking up the newspaper to take it home?

Joyce gave Lynette the newspaper. Roy and Billy carried in the house the missing fishing pole bag, along with the tackle box and note. The men were delighted. Roy was checking each hook and sinker and all the fishing whatnots in the tackle box like a child and its newly found toy.

Slowly the day finally ended. Everyone had left for home taking their Christmas gifts with them, except Roy and Joyce who were going home around noon on Sunday.

Lynette started to help Joyce pack for their trip back home when she stopped. "Why do you bring all those clothes back and forth? Check what you need to take back home and leave the rest in the guest room." It was agreed.

Roy came into the guest room; he wanted to watch the three stooges on the DVD he brought with him from home to play on this TV. Lynette and Joyce played scrabble at the kitchen table till past midnight. Joyce began to have difficulty in spelling words from being sleepy. Lynette was happily winning at scrabble, a game that she hardly ever won with Joyce who was an ace speller. The game ended when Joyce accidently knocked the box off the table with the letter tiles scattering on the floor. "I am sorry, Mother," Joyce said with tears in her eyes, feeling like a child again.

Lynette gave Joyce a kiss on her cheek, "I will pick these up. Go to bed. I love you." Joyce whispered, "Me too."

Chapter 15

It was four in the morning, and Lynette was so fidgety she could not stay still. Rather than lying in bed any longer, she got up and dressed. Not wanting to make any noise for fear of waking either Joyce or Roy, who did not need to get up before nine or ten in the morning, Lynette decided to drive to the beach and sit in her car until it became light enough to see where she was stepping on the sand. Lynette had a fear of stepping on a hermit crab. She saw a couple of them during the day, and they looked like prehistorical monsters with huge teeth and claws.

Soon she was walking down to the edge of the sand; the water felt cool and slippery where the waves were lapping at her legs with the incoming tide. A manatee caught her eye. She stopped walking, stared out to sea, smiling as she saw about three manatees jumping up out of the water, then diving into the water playing with each other. Lynette continued to look out at the water while slowly walking. She saw two fishing boats at a distance traveling at a rapid speed, causing large waves splashing against the sides of the boats, and circling toward the shore getting lost with the tide. She wondered where the fishing boats were going to anchor. Perhaps the fishing boats were on their way to pick up the people who would spend their day or days on these boats. She had never been able to ride on a boat, for she had motion sickness at various movements of the waves, amusement park rides, and sometimes even in an automobile, except when she was the driver. However, she felt envious of the fun these people were going to have.

Lynette looked at her watch—hanging from a chain on her neck. It was still early, only seven, the time she usually arrived at the beach. She enjoyed watching the sun rise and felt a bit guilty not sharing it with Jay. *Where did he disappear to?*

Lynette had walked further this morning than she had ever walked before and was not tired, but knew she had to turn around and start walking back to where she started, which now was quite a distance. Lynette began reliving yesterday in her mind and was smiling at the memories. It had been a busy day with all fifteen of them not counting her three great-grandchildren who were at the small table. Actually, only one child aged five was at the table.

The one-year-old was in the high chair, and the third child—a mere baby of nine months—was in the playpen near the small table. Lynette was glad to see Belinda and Erick mix in with her children as if they knew each other all their lives.

It was funny to see the name cards switched around from where Lynette had arranged them on the table. Well, if they were happier at different seats, she was too. Ruth had taken her mother aside and explained it was not where they were to sit but what they were to sit on; no one really wanted to sit on the folding chairs.

Just as Lynette poured her second glass of wine, she heard mumbling about Chester. Lynette eyed her daughter Ruth, who said, "Don't look at me. It was Billy who yapped to everyone about meeting Chester."

It was Billy's turn to get the hot seat; he volunteered. "I was asked who was the man in our photo on the wall. I had to answer, 'Did you want me to say he was a stranger who sat at our table?' Come on, be real!"

Soon there was friendlier bickering as in most families where one got teased, but somehow it all seemed to be about Lynette and her boyfriend Chester. The doorbell rang, and a hush came over everyone. Billy suggested it might be Chester; immediately all eyes were on Billy. Roy, being the closest to the door, opened it, "Nobody is here. Wait, there is a blue car driving out the driveway." Roy ran out the porch door to take a better look at the car. "Well, well, look what was dropped off? Flowers for you, Mother," he said, handing the large poinsettia plant to Lynette. It was too heavy for her, and Roy still held the plant as he helped her to set it on the table. Lynette looked, but there was no card to show the name of the person who had sent the flowers. What's even more strange was that there was no name of the florist delivering the flowers.

Billy said, "I think it was Chester who dropped the poinsettia in the driveway. No florist would do that. The rule is to make sure the right person gets the flowers. Remember Roy mentioned a blue car. Chester has a blue Impala Chevy. He probably wanted to give them to you but saw all the cars and chickened out. I wish he would have come in for a few minutes. Guys, I want you to know he is a hell of a good fellow. We hit it off great, as if I knew Chester all my life." Billy liked the limelight; talking about something no one else knew made him feel important somehow.

It was agreed that Chester should be asked to come to Tampa for Christmas Day. Lynette asked, "Where is he to stay? He has no money for a hotel."

Billy answered, "With five full bedrooms, we have enough room for an army to sleep over."

Lynette agreed to ask Chester to come with her to Tampa if he didn't have other plans. Lynette was happy when the conversation turned once more to Roy's fishing pole's travel; immediately there was no more talk about Chester.

Ruth later suggested she and her mother take a walk around the block a few times to work off the large meal. She used that as an excuse but wanted to be alone to talk with Lynette. She asked, "Are you sure you want to get more involved with Chester?"

Lynette explained a little more of their personal sex life, but admitting their relationship was not going any place. "He comes over, and we don't really even talk. We just have sex and a cup of coffee, and he is gone."

"Isn't that a rule of yours, not to go anywhere until you are sure of him? At least that is what you have been saying," stated Ruth.

"Before, that was true. But now that sex is good, I want to go out to a restaurant or club—and maybe dance—or even to a movie. He doesn't bring over a movie to even make a pretense of wanting to do anything but have sex," explained Lynette. She suddenly felt used, like Belinda warned her about. *There definitely had to be a long talk about how I felt with Chester,* she thought.

It seemed that as soon as the Ruth and her mother had returned home, everyone was ready to leave. Their excuse was that it was late, but Lynette wondered why everyone became so quiet and made a hasty exit. Roy said, "I am glad that is over. I would have rather gone fishing."

Joyce showed her mother another large poinsettia plant, which was placed on the table also with no card or name of florist.

Joyce said, "I am sorry for the confusion, but again the doorbell rang. By the time Roy was able to open the door, a van was pulling out of your driveway. He almost fell on this big plant."

Lynette jumped at the sound of the phone ringing. It was the clerk from Brooks Florist; she was sorry, but the card fell out of the order.

Lynette asked, "Why on earth would your driver just leave the Christmas plant outside the door?"

"I am sorry. He is not one of our regular drivers. We will give you a discount on your next order."

"You can just forget the next order. I would like to know the name of who sent the flowers to me," said Lynette.

"The card should read, 'With love, Sam and Sue,'" replied the clerk.

Later Joyce said, "I am sorry about all the talk about Chester. Maybe you should have invited him to your dinner party."

Lynette only replied, "Maybe he should have been here, but that is history. Who knows how long it will be before Chester will be history?" Those words left a sour taste in Lynette's mouth. She wondered why she was being so nasty to Joyce. Why was she killing the messenger? Suddenly Lynette laughed out loud as she walked on the beach remembering yesterday. Well, that was yesterday. She would apologize to Joyce when she got home. Today she was enjoying the beach. When she looked up, she realized she had walked past the footpath and was at the edge of the parking lot. Well, there was a lot on her mind.

Suddenly she heard a familiar voice calling her name. "Lynette! Lynette! Is that you, Lynette?" Lynette looked around. There at the wooden picnic table stood a tall man drinking something from a paper cup, which came from the nearby vendor. It was Jay! Lynette ran to him, giving Jay a tight bear hug.

"Miss me?"

"Did I ever! Where have you been?"

"I just got here and saw your car. Hopefully you are staying a little longer," Jay said.

"Darn it, I wish I could, but my daughter Joyce and son-in-law are sleeping. I don't want to cause them any concern about me if they wake up and find me gone. I am taking them to the airport where we will have breakfast before they fly back to New Jersey."

Jay was holding her hands. He said, "I had some family business to take care of. I might have to go back in a few days. What are your plans for the New Year's Eve?"

"At this moment, I don't know. But I am going to my daughter Ruth's house in Tampa on the afternoon of Christmas Eve and celebrate Christmas Day with my grandchildren. I will drive back home on the day after Christmas with my daughter Joyce and Roy. Geez, but it is good to see you again."

After they hugged, she ran to her car, opened the trunk, and took out her shoes. She leaned against the car to put her sandy feet into her shoes. She usually washed the sand off her legs and feet, but she forgot to do it when she saw Jay. It was too late now. She felt very dreamy driving home and had to force herself to concentrate on driving the back roads, with the hidden curves of the two-lane narrow roadway. Lynette feared these back roads. Too many teenage males thought they were cowboys with their spirited stallion galloping the grassy hills and open fields of yesteryear's badlands. Lynette knew sooner or later there will be a horrible accident and prayed it would not be involving her or anyone she knew or loved.

Chapter 16

Days flew by quickly. Lynette walked slowly on the beach, collecting seashells as she searched the shore for Jay, being delighted when she saw him. She now could recognize his tall lean body even at a distance; as soon as she saw him, she would start a fanatic waving of her arms and hands in the air.

Catching the sight of her always brought a smile to Jay's face, and he could not keep his long legs from running to her.

They now had coffee at the same vending machine that Lynette had earlier turned her nose up about before going home. She now knew he was single and in the process of selling his house in Maplewood. They both had a laughing fit when he told her he lived across from the Dome Building.

Lynette was alone at home but did not feel lonely even though she had not seen or heard from Chester since she made the stupid phone call the other day asking what his plans were for New Year's Eve. He became upset;

he would not tempt himself with all the drinking. He even questioned her on how she could be so uncaring to even ask him.

Belinda had phoned every day inquiring how Lynette was now that Chester wasn't coming around as much.

Lynette reminded Belinda that it is the Christmas holidays; Chester is probably busy shopping and mailing his packages back north. It is also a stressful time for Chester's daughter, Jenny, who is alone with her husband in the service.

Belinda asked, "What about your needs at this supposing merry party time with friends? You should be on his arm, and Jenny could have the other arm. Doesn't sound kosher to me."

Lynette replied, "It's okay. You forget I am going to be at Ruth's house during Christmas Eve, Christmas, and the day after. As a matter of fact, I will be busy with Joyce and Roy until January 2 when I will be driving Joyce and Roy back to the airport. You do know, Belinda, that we made plans for various shows as far back as last Christmas, and no ticket for Chester. Chester does not want to spend the money to see a live play because he claims it is too expensive. Besides, he claims he would rather watch the ball come down in New York on TV. In a way, I am glad Chester has Jenny to keep him occupied so he does not start chasing the ladies."

On December 28, a Friday morning, Lynette was enjoying breakfast in the Eggs Your Way Restaurant with Joyce and Roy. As a new waitress came to refill the coffee cups, Lynette moved her cup closer to the waitress when a movement caught her eye. Lynette turned her head in that direction and saw her favorite waitress, Gloria, laughing and talking as she walked toward a small table near the window; the customer with Gloria was Chester.

Lynette felt a sharp pull on her heart wondering if he saw her. Gloria stopped at Lynette's table as she was passing and wished everyone a wonderful holiday. *Gloria hung around the table a little longer than needed,* thought Lynette. *Was she looking for a Christmas tip?* The green-eyed monster had attacked Lynette, and she was annoyed with Gloria for being so friendly with Chester.

Roy whispered, "I thought she was going to sit down and eat with us the way she was hovering around." Lynette ignored the remarks; she was lost in her thoughts about Chester. Did he see her? He must have as he was sitting almost in her direction if he looked their way. Maybe it was on purpose to make her jealous. Was she supposed to acknowledge that she knew he was a few tables away joking with Gloria and enjoying every second? Gloria continued to kid with Chester as she cleaned the table next to him.

Lynette began to wonder if Chester was in his own way letting her know that he did not want to see her anymore. It would be totally embarrassing if she offered a seat at her table to him, and he refused. What would she say to Joyce and Roy?

Gloria came to Lynette's table again. This time she sat on the seat next to Lynette as she handed Lynette a piece of scrap paper. Lynette read the words, "He is pretending he does not see you. He is waiting for you to notice him. Please, he is so sweet."

Out loud, Gloria said, "I must get to work," and disappeared. Lynette and Joyce went to the bathroom. On the way back to their table, she looked at Chester looking at her in such a melancholy way; it melted her heart. Lynette asked, "Hey, you want to share our table?"

Chester picked up all his service items and coffee quickly. "I was waiting for your phone call. I got frantic and called you on the cell, but you never returned my call."

Lynette whispered, "I hardly ever hear the cell phone, let alone answer it. I use it for emergence only. Chester, I am sorry."

Joyce nudged Roy with her elbow, saying, "See, that is why I tell you to only call us on my cell phone. Forget dialing either of Mother's phones."

Chester blew his nose, began sniffing. He cleared his throat, "I called your house phone and got the busy signal. The operator said a phone was off the hook. Did you check all your phones?" Lynette shook her head and hunched her shoulders. She thought that may be the reason he didn't call, and with Joyce visiting, she had not given any thoughts to the phone not ringing or the answering machine not having any messages.

Chester scuffed his shoes on the floor; with his eyes looking down at his empty coffee cup, he said, "I took the chance you might be here. I looked kind of crazy driving around the parking lot searching for your car. I was afraid you might not be alone, or maybe you are tired of me, maybe I hurt your feelings somehow." He knew Lynette's daughter and son-in-law were listening to his every word. He needed to hear Lynette was not angry with him.

Lynette made a sour face. "Don't be silly! By the way, the poinsettia plant was beautiful. Still is. Why didn't you sign the card?"

"What poinsettia plant? I never gave you any flowers. Was I supposed to?"

Lynette was puzzled. "That wasn't you with the blue Chevy that left the large poinsettia plant in front of the porch screen door?"

"No!" Chester thought to himself it probably was from Pete or Quinton or some other jerk she had stashed away. He would have to watch her a little more closely.

Joyce said, "Is it possible the poinsettia was for one of your neighbors?" Lynette interrupted, "Oh well, it is mine now."

Chapter 17

Roy asked Chester if he had plans to go and celebrate the New Year's Eve. Chester explained how he had been an alcoholic all his life and just in the past few years has been dry and now cannot tolerate all the noise. The conversation changed to how recently Joyce and Roy had been here only to return for the Christmas holidays. Roy jerked his head toward Joyce. "She plans everything. I just go along, and many times Joyce is able to use the freebie miles. And our holidays and sick days must be used during the year, or they are lost."

Roy and Chester were happily chatting about sports and how maybe the two of them would get together for a day of fishing on one of the all-day fishing boats. Lynette overheard Chester say, "The girls can go shopping, and we can do some deep fishing."

Nothing came of any of Chester's conversations. Joyce asked if Roy wanted her mother to phone Chester to remind him of their fishing getaway promises; however, Roy would not allow that. Soon their Christmas vacation was over.

CHAPTER 18

Lynette waved to Joyce and Roy a last good-bye until they returned in spring. Her cell phone rang while she was leaving the airport; normally, she did not answer the cell phone unless she was parked. She did not want any distractions while driving. Lynette answered the cell in case it was from Joyce or Roy.

She heard Chester's voice, "Where are you?"

"I just left the airport on my way home. Today is January 2. The vacation is over. Roy was really disappointed not going deep fishing with you. What happened?"

"A flu bug had me in bed a few days. I will make it up to Roy another time."

"Chester, are you okay now?"

"I will be if I can see you. I will meet you in your driveway," he said.

Lynette was glad there was almost no traffic, and she drove as fast as she could hopping to get home before Chester as she mentally thought of how messy the house was.

Chester dozed off in his car in her driveway while waiting for Lynette to come home. He hit his head on the steering wheel when he was startled from the honking of Lynette's automobile horn.

"I am glad you waited. Now we can start the New Year off right," she said. Chester slowly got out of his car. *He looks disappointed,* she thought. She said, "I am starved. Want to go to the Dome to eat? I have a coupon to buy one meal and get the second one for half price. We can split the cost."

Chester suggested they have sex first, then go to the Dome, and eat an early supper. He could not get in the mood for anything but a quick act of sex. Afterward, he knew he left her with a lot to be desired. He felt she had to suffer a little for being so hurtful, leaving him alone on New Year's Eve while she partied. Maybe she will now realize she was in the wrong. He had earlier told her how lonely he was on New Year's Eve. Her answer was, "Sweetheart, we asked you to come and celebrate with us. You refused."

"Why didn't you call me and let me know you were going out only for a late dinner? I would have joined you. I was curious about the new restaurant," Chester said.

Lynette thought he was whining, best not to say a word about the good time they had. He was not missed at the party, and this time the sex was almost the worst that she could remember. Lynette walked in the bathroom shutting out his voice; she would take her shower and let him complain without her.

Lynette did not think the subject should be discussed anymore and asked, "Are we still going to the Dome to grab a bite to eat?"

Chester said, "Yes!" He sat on the couch while she dressed in light pink shorts and bright hot pink T-shirt. When she stepped into the parlor, he thought she looked good, too good for the Dome, and yet he didn't want to spend any money on her. If she can afford to spend over fifty bucks on a dinner, she could just pay the ten dollars for her share at the Dome.

Lynette picked up her pink flowered handbag. "I am ready. Your car or mine?"

Chester rose up from the couch looking at her tanned skin. Then he looked away, making a frown. "Lynette, I am sorry, but could we skip this? I want to go home and lie down. All of a sudden I feel like I am getting sick again, maybe a relapse. You better take an extra vitamin C. I will not even kiss you, no need for you to be sick. You look exceptionally pretty. You go ahead and enjoy yourself without me."

Lynette felt blown away. True, their sex was no good for her again. Still, she wanted someone to go for a walk and play ball with in the pool, even watch TV in the parlor or on a set in her bedroom. But it was not going to be Chester, she was beginning to realize. Lately there were many times she wished Chester had Jay's personality.

After Chester left, she drove to the Dome, ordered a cheeseburger and Coors Light beer, even french fries. She let her mind drift from Chester to Jay. She wanted to go somewhere with Jay to have coffee, not from the vending machine. Just the two of them and not all sandy, but of course, she could never let Jay know for fear he would run away. Now he was gone anyway!

Chapter 19

On January 6, Gloria was all a flutter at seeing Lynette in her working area. "I think I blew it for you with Chester. I just thought you all went out to that fancy nightclub. My brother said he joined you and the others at your table on New Year's Eve. I sort of mentioned how much fun my brother had, and I teased him about losing you if he was not careful. I was dumb-blasted when Chester said he was home all alone."

"I went out with my daughter Joyce and her husband, Roy, to the new nightclub, we asked if he wanted to join us, but he would not have anything to do with going anywhere there was an alcoholic beverage. Don't let it bother you. Chester could not afford it anyway. Gloria, your brother came without a date, and the owner asked if your brother could join us. I had a ball!"

Later that night, Belinda stopped over at Lynette's house. After a few drinks, Lynette told of her lies about sex with Chester; she also confessed she didn't know why but had told Ruth the truth of their sexuality. Belinda was disappointed in not being told long time ago of what was happening. Now that she had, Belinda advised Lynette to drop Chester.

The following two days, Chester made sex to the delight of Lynette. During their cuddling afterward, on January 9, Lynette asked about the Band-Aid on his groin.

Chester explained, "I had no sores of any kind on my body, but the Band-Aid was a sex patch. It works like the little blue pill that everyone talks about for men. You know, Viagra!"

Lynette asked, "Why don't you use them all the time?"

"They cost too much," Chester said, "especially at the end of the month or like now when I am under the weight of a lot of holiday bills. I was going to ask you for help to pay for them, but I was not sure of what you may think."

"You thought right, Chester. There is no way I would even think about paying for those sex aids for you."

Long after he left for home, she was thinking and fuming of how he had acted by using those patches to enhance his penis. Chester put a lot of blame on her when, in actuality, it was he who could not get it up. And he was too cheap to want to give her the full enjoyment because his penis was too limp, before the use of the sexual patch.

Lynette remembered one night he had not been able to complete the sex act and Chester asked if she had any toys. Yes, she did have one sexual toy but would not let Chester know about it. If she used it while he was here, then why would she need him? Therefore, she let him think she did not have or use any sexual aids.

He did not come for a few days nor even call to explain his distance. Lynette felt it was time to call Chester and let him go; it was no good for either of them. Belinda's advice was beginning to sink in about saying adios to Chester, but it was too hard to do. Instead of calling Chester, she phoned Ruth and brought her up-to-date of her affair with Chester and what Belinda had advised her to do.

Unknown to either of them, Billy had picked up the phone to use it and heard his wife and her mother talking about dumping Chester. He listened to find the reason but had picked up the phone after most of the conversation was over. He apologized for overhearing them on the phone and agreed with Ruth that Lynette should be nice—and let Chester go and find someone who will want him—and not be used.

Lynette knew he did not hear all the conversation and said, "You are right. I will call Chester tomorrow morning. I just do not have the nerve tonight."

Billy thought he knew what the problem was with Chester and his mother-in-law. Later that night after the phone call, he said, "Ruth, honey, I understand what is bugging your mother more than you know."

Ruth wondered just how much he heard when he eavesdropped on the phone. She sucked in her breath asking, "Tell me what you think is the reason my mother wants out of this affair."

"Anyone can see. Chester is looking for an intimate relationship, but your mother is looking for a companion, which at her age is understandable. Just listening to Chester talk of his life, I got the feeling he has been in and out of sexual relationships. I even wondered if I should say something to him, but I kept my mouth shut. But if I were in Chester's shoes, I would like someone to be up-front and not fool around with my heart and feelings like your mother has been doing. You may not know it, but she is a flirt. Maybe she doesn't know how she talks and acts. I know she is innocent, but Chester may be thinking she is ready for everything, and anything goes." He was now smiling for being able to foretell how that situation was long before anyone else knew or suspected trouble.

Ruth licked her top lip with her tongue to keep from laughing; her sweet Billy didn't hear their phone conversation after all.

Chapter 20

On January 15, Lynette got enough nerve to speak to Chester. As she dialed his number, her hands trembled. She listened to the phone ring and heard his voice, "Hello!"

She almost hung up the phone. "Hi! Chester, I have not heard from you. We need to talk."

Lynette was interrupted. "I have been going through hell these last few days. I am glad you phoned. Lynette, I have to go back home immediately. My stepfather has died of a heart attack. He suffered a stroke and never recovered while in the emergency room."

Lynette was dumbstruck. She felt guilty, choking on her unspoken words. "Chester, my love, what you have been going through these past few days, I cannot even imagine. I should be by your side."

"No, no! I should have called you. It is just getting my house taken care of so I can drive up north. My mom needs me. We are all in shock by Dad's death. He was the healthy one and has been my mom's caretaker, as well as the love of her life for the last several years. Mom is in her midnineties and frail. I don't know what this is doing to her. Dad was several years younger than Mom. I can't believe what has happened. This is such a shock."

"Chester, please let me go up north with you and give you the comfort you need to be able to help your mother. I can be ready to leave by tomorrow." Lynette was already packing in her mind what to take with her and closing up her house. Maybe even have Billy do what had to be done to the house that would take more time than she had. Her place was with Chester now in his moment of need and sorrow. No wonder he did not call her. At this moment, she wanted to take him in her arms and soothe all his pain away.

"Wait, Lynette, please," she heard him say. "I will not need you to come with me. I am having a limousine take me to the airport in a couple of hours. I will not need you in Indiana. I have a neighbor whom I have known for several years. I will be helped and comforted by my neighbor Gene. We have been intimate for at least six or more years, so you do not need to come with me. Mom would not understand our relationship. She has just recently accepted my relationship with Gene."

"You never told me about her?"

"Oh, Lynette, my neighbor is not a woman. Gene is my dearest friend. You are the first woman I ever felt anything for since my divorce years ago. I thought I told you I am bisexual."

Lynette was now in shock. He never mentioned his sexual ways. How would she know? She did not want to think. How could he do this to her? Chester was still talking on the phone; it was difficult to take in what he was saying. There was a painful sob caught in her throat as she heard him say, "Gene will most likely take care of all my needs, and he is now at my mother's house being a caregiver, which is my job. I must go now. I want you to understand that I am grateful for all you have given me. Someday I will be back in this area again, and I know we will be together. Be patient with me. Remember, I still have my condo, which I just bought because I wanted to be near you. For now I will be renting it furnished. Would you know of anyone who wants to rent?"

Chester never got to finish his sentence as Lynette had hung up the phone.

She now thought she knew why their sex act was so often incomplete.

Chester was only interested in oral sex with her, but he did try, she knew that. Still, she ached for Chester and what they tried to be.

Lynette knew she had to change her life, and it was not Chester that was really leaving her; she was going to dump him with the phone call.

Chapter 21

A couple of weeks had gone by, and she was lonely. Lynette did not tell anyone about the last phone call she had with Chester. She let everyone think she had broken up their relationship as planned.

Lynette drove to the beach but did not get out of her car. She tried to think of how she would get her ideas organized; travel sounded good but not by herself. Now that Chester was gone, who would she go with? However, he never had any money, and she had no intentions to pay for his share. A loud thump startled Lynette; she smiled at the young girl who was leaning over the hood of the car reaching for the Frisbee that had landed there.

"I am so sorry! We should not be fooling around in the parking lot when there's a big sandy beach a few steps away," the girl said.

Lynette opened the car door, still looking at the girl who was in her early teens. She looked at her car; seeing no dents or paint scraped, she shooed off the girl. "Join your friends, but don't play in the parking lot!" Lynette watched the girl run with her friends down the footpath, feeling strangely protective of the girl, wishing to mother her, to watch her grow. She shook her head. *Now what?* Lynette wondered. *I better just sit at the picnic table before I get myself involved in something I may be sorry for.*

Chapter 22

Just then, a soft hand touched her shoulder; she heard a lady say, "A penny for your thoughts. You had the most pensive look on your face, as if you were in deep thought of something desirous yet sad."

Laughing for the first time in a few days, Lynette felt a connection with this woman. "Watching that girl reminded me of my girls at her age. I also thought about how my companion had promised to teach me to play golf one day, but he died, and I never learned."

"Sorry to hear of your loss. Was it sudden?"

Lynette rolled her eyes, hunching her shoulders, raising her arms to explain. "No. I . . . Why did I even say anything about my companion Tony? He passed away a few years ago. He no longer was able to do anything, let alone play golf. He was brain demented the last few years of his life. He died of heart failure." The woman had quietly sat next to Lynette. Lynette could not stop from babbling. She has been accused of idle prattle, but carrying on with this stranger about her personal feelings was unbelievable. The woman offered a bottle of water, which Lynette grabbed to stop from talking; she chugalugged the liquid so swiftly that a bubble came to her throat. She darn near choked to death, or so she thought. If only she could burp with the pain now in her chest, which was also burning. She lightly hit her chest with her clenched fist trying to swallow the air bubble caught in her esophagus. The woman pulled Lynette up to a standing position and lightly patted her on her back like a baby; Lynette immediately started to laugh. A loud burp was heard as it eased from her throat. "Wow, that was something!" chirped Lynette.

"Better out than in," said the woman.

"Yes, you are so right. It still hurts a bit, but now I am okay." The woman, offering her hand, said, "My name is Amy."

Lynette clasped the woman's hand. "My name is Lynette. I know you are too busy to hear the story of my life, but I just broke up with a dear friend. To be honest, he became dearer when we broke up. It just brought me back to some of the dreams I once had, but not enough to put any effort in them."

Amy was now listening earnestly to Lynette's many plans: how she wanted to play golf, the piano, guitar, to travel, but wants a partner to share her life. Amy said, "This chance meeting between us is eerie, to say the least. But I think it is fate. Listen to what I have to say, and you will understand what I mean." Lynette was happy to have someone else take over the conversation; she intended to listen to every word Amy expressed. Amy continued, "My cousin owns an adult dating club. The men want a woman who is close to their age for companionship, maybe marriage."

"I do not want to get married!"

"Please, Lynette, listen. No one is telling you to get married, but these men who are up in age do not want to go searching at bars or local clubs. They are ready to settle down, and most of them have enough money to spend on the lady. Of course, they are not looking for a gold digger, but someone to share their life with. Maybe do some traveling. That is something I heard you say you were interested in, why not give it a chance?" Amy explained how some of the gentlemen do not want to go on the second date and don't give a reason. "They are very lonely. I could use any helpful information for their portfolio that you could give us. Maybe help yourself at the same time."

Lynette was amused enough to think about it, even smiled at the idea. "But what kind of a man would do this form of advertisement?"

"There is a gentleman who is retired, wants to meet a senior female golfer. You should call him." Amy opened her huge handbag searching for something. Lynette thought Amy was looking for a pencil and paper. Within a few minutes, Amy gave Lynette a folded blue brochure; it was turned to the classified section. "See that ad? Call the number, and this is my phone number that is written here." She had pointed at a number written in red ink.

Lynette whispered, "I don't know how to play golf. Do you think he would take the time to teach me?" She wondered how much a set of golf clubs would cost. *Could I learn at my age?*

"I see no reason why he wouldn't want to do anything to please you if he is interested in you. We already know he is lonely and looking."

"Okay. Nothing ventured, nothing gained!"

"That is the spirit! Call me later. I want to know how you two get along. Tell me everything, and I mean everything! If he does not work out, I have a few more names for you. These men pay to join, and if they connect with the woman, the club gets a significant fee. But there are not enough senior women. Lynette, you will be having fun and getting paid for giving me firsthand information on what you think about the men. Please say you will do it." Looking at her watch, she said, "I have to go now." They hugged each other and walked to their own cars.

In her car, Lynette wondered just what was she thinking to promise to call this stranger. *Am I brave enough to call this man? As soon as I walk in the door, I will call him.* After she did, she was delighted to hear him say he wanted to talk more, but was busy at the moment. *This is too good,* she thought and laughed out loud. She knew the saying that if it sounds too good to be true, it was. After all, there was no such thing as a free lunch; you must pay somehow.

Chapter 23

It was February 9, a Saturday, and the meeting place was at Eggs Your Way Restaurant. Aldo was in his late seventies and, unbeknown to Lynette, was a friend of the manager's husband; seems they had discussed Lynette's character, and everything Aldo heard about Lynette, he liked. He saw Lynette a few times without her knowing after she was pointed out to him. Now to meet her in person, he was nervous. So was Lynette, but she did not show it. He was very shy and clumsy; he knocked over the glass of water, which spilled on the table running off on to Lynette's lap. Both of them were trying to quickly sop up the water. Lynette laughed as she saw Aldo blush. Lynette said, "Good thing it is not winter weather, or this ice would be my death from pneumonia."

He had offered to buy her a new outfit or have hers dry-cleaned. She exclaimed, "These are washable shorts. I will change when I get home." There was more talk as they sat in the booth at the back by themselves for almost two hours. Lynette found him very interesting and a bragger, possibly a liar. She would go out with him a few days and see if he was a keeper.

It was Valentine's Day when Lynette called Amy. "Amy, it will not work out with Aldo. Do you want me to go into the details?"

Amy was disappointed but wanted to hear it all—but in a digested fashion. Lynette said, "You ask me about Aldo. I will tell it as it happened. He was into golf but did not want to play it anymore. He is looking for a homebody who will spend almost twenty-four hours with him. My family could join us, but I doubt if he really means that. He probably said the same words to his two ex-wives about his stepchildren. Now he can't stand the mention of them, let alone the sight of them. He worked too many hours and played golf in his spare time, was not with his family as he probably should have been. He does not care. He says he did the best that he could at the time. Now he wants to spend his later years with someone who has the same interest as he has. Most important is he does not want to be out in a restaurant and have any male come to the table to say hello to him or me, just thinking this man may have slept with me. Amy, he is very outspoken in what he wants and doesn't want."

"Lynette, what does he look like?"

"He is a gentleman, not especially handsome. He was rough-looking, short in stature, and muscular. He took me to his house, or should I say mansion? The house has a complete gym, with a complete bathroom and spa or a hot tub next to the gym. There are five bedrooms with a complete bathroom in each one and a sitting room next to the master bedroom. He said he could make one of the bedrooms into a den or library, which I could use for whatever I desire.

His kitchen is state-of-the-art, yet he seldom entertains there and does not like to."

Amy wrote down what Lynette was saying in shorthand wishing she had just used the recorder but didn't have any new tape. Amy would add this information to Aldo's file folder.

Lynette continued, "Aldo is in his late seventies, looks to be older than that with a sort of large head and flat face. It is like his head is too big for his frame. He can fly an airplane from the nearby airport. I was surprised to see he has a pilot license. Somehow he was just bragging so much that I did not believe him. If he has all this, why would he want me—an old lady who is fat and neither fashionable nor sociable?"

Amy said, "In his folder it is listed that he has worked all his life in various business of his own, from building houses to running a trucking business, a trucking equipment business, then had marital problems and sold them. He was married twice, never had any children, but each wife had one son. It states he has money, and his credit report lists him to have 850-plus rating, which is the best you can have."

Lynette took a deep breath and said, "Aldo is a spender without thinking. He found out I was interested in seashells. We went to a shell factory, and there was this huge conch shell that caught my eye. He wanted to give it to me. Amy, it cost $200, I refused it. Aldo wants me to move in with him to be able to see if I can be happy with him. He wanted to know this on our third date, which was at his house. He has a gardener, who also is his driver. The housekeeper is also the cook, and she hires other staff that is needed. They take care of everything. The meal was divine. I think they are a couple, and they have living quarters in an apartment above the garage. He says I can keep my house for my children to use as a holiday house. Aldo says we are too old to wait. He does not want to use any of my assets. I should put them in a trust. He will take care of me and all my wants. I can't make up my mind so quickly. We do not know each other. This guy scares the hell out of me. He moves too fast. I asked what happens if he finds out I am not what he is looking for, what then? Amy, he had me checked out before we met in person! Amy, he even told me he may not be able to have sex, but he would make me happy however in any way he could."

"Lynette, what are you trying to tell me?"

"Aldo is a man who can move mountains with his connections. He has too much money for me and my values. He gives off the attitude that money buys everything. I get the idea he wants to buy me. Then regardless what I say, he will own me. I can't do that, I wish I could. I hope you understand."

"Have you broke it off already without giving Aldo a fair chance?"

Lynette was now walking around with the portable phone wishing she never met Aldo. "I lied to Aldo. I told him I was seeing someone else before I met him and have decided to go back with my friend as we have more in common with each other than Aldo and I have." Amy interrupted, "My god, what did he say?"

Lynette brushed back a tear "Amy, he didn't say a word. At first, he fidgeted with something in his lap, never looking at me. He just stood up and threw a hundred-dollar bill on the table, then turned, and walked out of the restaurant. I was embarrassed and felt I crushed his feelings. I also felt all eyes were on me. I am so sorry. I did not want to lead him on. No telling what he might do later on, that's why I broke it off. But I could tell he was fuming. I think I will just forget about men. I must do something else with my life."

Chapter 24

Amy said, "Wait, Lynette, I have a few folders of men that are hard to find that special lady. I would really appreciate your help. You are being paid for not only your time but also for all your expense—even special outfits if you need them. And remember you just may find the man of your dreams!"

Lynette was curious and excited. "Yes, I could do that. We could meet in the open on the patio outside of Books a Million. There are tables where we could have coffee. I could even read a magazine while I wait for this fellow."

Lynette was given the first names of three men and their phone numbers, nothing else as Amy wanted to get fresh information to see why the men never seemed to find a partner to keep even for a repeat date.

It was easier now for Lynette to call the men as she felt it was like being a reporter, interviewing and meeting someone new, maybe a keeper.

Charles Moran was in his late seventies, quite handsome, and a womanizer; he gave every woman he saw a once-over even when he was with Lynette. Charles did not seem to care if Lynette noticed him looking or not. Earlier when Lynette mentioned she felt funny when he was checking out other woman in her presence, his answer was, "Well, I am not dead yet."

Charles had explained his retirement funds were eaten up by his three ex-wives, and he would need a part-time job for the rest of his life. He was looking for someone to share the expense of everyday living. Charles explained he wanted a companion who was a looker and had enough money to help ease the crunch of his failed finances. He just wanted someone to share his rented home; he was not looking for anything but friendship. However, if friendship turned out to be a more tender, loving relationship, that would be okay. But most important is she had to be someone he could enjoy looking at every morning without a lot of makeup plastered all over her face.

Lynette was nervously sitting at one of the back tables wishing she had something in her hands. Suddenly, Charles suggested, "How about I go inside and order a cup of their gourmet coffee?"

"That would be great, and something sweet if they have it," answered Lynette, feeling relieved.

Charles came back to the table empty-handed. "The coffee urn was being cleaned, and when fresh coffee is made, a waitress will bring it out to us. I left the pastry up to her choosing. She said she knew you and what you liked."

Lynette found that odd as she hardly had a friend, and the only waitresses she knew worked at Eggs Your Way Restaurant. "I wonder who that could be." After a few minutes, the door to the patio opened, and carrying a tray toward her table was Gloria. "What are you doing here?" cried Lynette, almost choking on her words. Lynette had chosen this meeting place because it was in a public place, and no one she knew would see her to ask any questions; now her favorite waitress was serving the coffee.

Gloria was all smiles as she explained, "I am only working here part-time. I need more hours than I am given at Eggs Your Way. The tips are better here too."

Charles was flirting outrageously with Gloria, which annoyed Lynette. Lynette introduced them but did not explain why they were together.

Gloria asked, "Where is Chester? I have not seen him in a while." This was a simple question, but Lynette almost spilled her coffee. With a hot red burning face, she said, "Chester had to go back up north. He had a family emergency. I don't expect to be seeing him around here in a long time, if ever."

Gloria left them alone, but not for long as she kept returning to their table to refill the cups with fresh coffee and wiping off the nearby tables while carrying on a conversation of small talk, mostly with Charles. Lynette felt as if she was not there. *What was going on here?* she wondered.

Charles asked, "Do you have the check ready?"

"Yes, it is in my pocket."

Charles looked at the bill. Lynette reached for her handbag to get her wallet, but she heard Charles say, "I have it!" Charles placed two bills on the table over the check and waved his finger in the air at Gloria for her to come to the table.

Gloria saw the cash on the check, walked slowly over to the table, picked up the cash, looking puzzled at Charles. She spread out the two bills. "I think you made a mistake," she said.

Charles, smiling, said, "No. I want you to keep the change."

Gloria's eyes were opened wide, and she stared at Lynette. Lynette looked at the check, which was made out for less than twenty dollars, gulped at the amount Charles was leaving for a tip. She said, "Take it. Charles wants you to have it."

Gloria, looking now at Charles, asked, "Are you sure? There is a twenty- and a ten-dollar bill here. Your check is for only $18.65. That's too much money."

Charles picked up the ten-dollar bill from the table saying, "Does that make you feel better?" Gloria was standing close to Charles; she nodded her head with a smile and winked at Lynette. With a swift movement, Charles had stuck the ten-dollar bill in Gloria's apron pocket. She opened her mouth to protest. Charles said, "It is for your extrafriendly service." He gently rubbed her apron pocket where the money was put. He added, "I wish I could do more for you."

Afterward, as Charles stood by Lynette's car, he asked, "How much do you know about Gloria?"

"She is single, if that is what you are asking. Other than that, I don't know anything about her. Why do you want to know?"

Without a thought given to Lynette, he said, "I would like to really get to know Gloria a lot more. Her youth and vitality is beckoning me."

"I tell you what. Suppose I give your phone number to Gloria and leave it up to her to decide if she wants to know you better?" She could see Charles was now interested in Gloria more than he ever was or could be in herself. It was definitely the age; Amy was introducing Charles to older women.

Later that day, Lynette went to Eggs Your Way Restaurant on the shift that Gloria was working. Lynette explained all about Charles and that he had wanted to date Gloria to see where it may go.

Later that night, Lynette related it all to Amy on the phone. "Damn, I wonder if I can send Charles a bill for the introduction of Gloria," said Amy.

Lynette left her phone number on the answering machine of George Bennett. She was hungry and wanted to see how Gloria and Charles were doing. For a couple of days, it seemed Gloria had vanished from both jobs where she was waitressing, yet Lynette knew Gloria needed the money. Tonight Lynette planned on asking someone about Gloria if she was not working on this shift, but there was Gloria looking happier than Lynette ever saw her look before. Gloria was on her way home but sat at Lynette's table.

"I can't thank you enough for introducing me to Charles. We are getting married," Gloria burst out loudly without regard to all who heard her. Lynette could not believe her ears. "I did not know Charles was the marrying kind."

"I moved in his apartment, which is bigger than my furnished one room."

"You don't know him. Aren't you rushing things a little?"

"Charles wants us to live together for a few months to see how compatible we are. If we can survive each other, we will get married. He loves me, and I adore him. I know there is an age difference, but I am not getting any younger."

"I only wanted to know if you were okay with Charles. I am happy for you, and I pray you will always be as happy as you are right now," said Lynette.

Lynette returned to her empty house and wished she could have only half of the enjoyment Gloria was having. She noticed there was a missed phone message on the answering machine; it was George. She dialed his number and immediately liked his deep-sounding voice.

They had agreed to meet at Eggs Your Way Restaurant; it no longer was a problem if anyone saw her with a strange man.

The following night, Lynette told the hostess to show George to her table when he came in. "He is already here," replied the hostess. "He is sitting at your favorite table. I gave him that table when he mentioned he was waiting for you."

Lynette checked him out as she walked to the table without the hostess. She sat down and acknowledged him. "I am Lynette. I see you were given my special table. Everyone knows I enjoy this table. I can see what is going on in the parking lot and all over the restaurant."

George was a very handsome man. She noticed he was tall and could not miss his bald head. As she looked closer, she noticed he had shaved his head, at least the sides.

He said, "I hope my bald head does not put you off. I have been assured I look better bald than with a few wisp of hair." He had seen her staring at his head.

Laughing, Lynette said, "I see your favorite hat. I take it for granted you were in the marines from the emblem," as she pointed to his cap on the table with the emblem facing her.

George explained all about his wants and his life—including the fact that he was married and had no plans to divorce his wife who was in a nursing home with Alzheimer's disease, with no chance of her getting better.

"Why are you looking for a partner at the agency?"

"I don't want to be alone anymore," he simply stated as if it was a normal thing to do. *Doesn't everyone?*

Lynette was confused and said so. George explained how he was not very ambitious during his youth; it was his wife who had the career.

He always was in between jobs, but his wife enjoyed him being the home keeper with her meals prepared. He had done all the wifely chores, including the bill paying, which his wife hated doing. If he were to get a divorce, he would lose everything and become penniless.

Lynette said, "You never mentioned that you still are married. I understand you were supposed to be a widower."

"Would you want to know me if I wrote I was still married?" he asked.

Lynette understood what he was saying but did not think any woman would want to get involved with a man who already said he was a taker. Maybe that was what his wife wanted, but he didn't want to be with his wife, only her finances. This was a tidbit that Amy would be glad to know about. The meal was long over, and they were still sipping coffee. Lynette wished it was a glass of wine.

George was quiet just trying to read what Lynette was thinking. Finally he asked, "So what is your decision? Do we go on from here getting to know each other, or are you still looking for the forever after?"

"I am not looking for marriage, but if I was going to be with someone, I want it to be something more than a fill-in person."

George stood up. "I understand. Take care of yourself, Lynette."

Lynette sat there wondering what she was doing going out with strange men. Why should she condemn him? She also was not being completely truthful. If the truth was known, she was simply a lonely old lady looking for a chance for a youthful romance. She should grow up and get on with life. She should be glad she was still healthy and get active in a travel club, with others her same age looking just to enjoy each day with whatever comes her way. Yes, she thought, she would join a travel club tomorrow.

At home it was late. Still, Lynette phoned Amy. She left a message, "No more men. By the way, George is married with his wife in a nursing home."

She hung up the phone; walking away, she heard it ring but had no intention of answering.

Chapter 25

It was Easter Sunday. Lynette did not go to church, too many families or couples even if they were mostly elderly in her church. The fact was, everyone seemed to have a partner; she was alone, and that was something she had to get use to.

Lynette drove to the beach as she walked on what could be her private beach; she was in deep thought. She was glad she had joined the senior travel club. At first, she hesitated to join for fear of being the extra female, but she was assured there would be far more single women than couples or single men. She would be in a group and be assigned a travel mate; of course, it would be a female, which she hoped would end up being close travel friends, going on many trips around the world or just in her own town.

One thing for sure, there was not going to be any more of her being on display of being rejected by some strange man she may not even want to know better. However, all these thoughts brought back her feelings for Chester and Jay.

After tiring herself from the long walk on the sandy beach, Lynette stood in front of the vending machine. She could even smell the hot chocolate she stood so close to. She had no money on her, but her purse with money was in the car. Lynette hoped there was the right amount of change and not a five- or twenty-dollar bill. If she put in an amount larger than a one-dollar bill, would the machine keep her change? she wondered. She slowly shook her head from side to side, while softly chewing her finger. With her hands in the pockets of her shorts, she walked to her car. All of a sudden, she realized her keys were not in her pockets. Frantically, she searched each pocket, no keys. She raised her head and looked in the direction of the picnic tables. Did she leave the keys there?

Oh my god, there was a man standing near the table she had been sitting at when she first came to the beach today. Should she wait till he was gone? No, she would go and look for her car keys; maybe he saw them. Once more, she looked in the car's window trying to see all over inside the car. She did not want to be a fool. No sight of her keys. She looked at the table again; the man had gone away. Running toward the picnic table, she tripped over a tree root, falling down, landing on her knees.

Lynette heard a male voice whisper, "Are you looking for these?" He was holding a set of keys in his fingers. She looked closer as she stood up. Were her eyes playing a trick on her? This man looked like someone she should know, but who?

Chapter 26

Lynette was so pleased to find her keys; she could now unlock the car's doors and locate her purse. Taking the keys from the outstretched hand, she turned to walk to her car; her brain registered that this man was Jay! She quickly turned back toward Jay.

Jay said, "Are you sleepwalking or dreaming about something interesting? I have been calling your name, but you did not look in my direction."

Lynette was flustered and stuttering, "I . . . I . . . I want . . . wanted something to . . . to drink. I lost my . . . my keys. You . . . you found them." Tears started to fall down her cheeks. Why was she crying? She didn't know.

Jay put his arms around her. She was safe now. *But for how long?* she wondered. Would he stay or disappear like before? Lynette needed to know even if what she heard was not what she wanted to hear.

"Are you staying?"

"Do you want me to?" Jay asked.

Lynette threw away her pride. "I have looked for you every day. I missed you more than I could ever tell you."

Jay was still holding Lynette in his arms; he bent his head kissing her gently on her forehead. "Funny. I was here almost every day looking for you. I came here this morning on Easter no less, just hoping to get a glimpse of you. You will never know the joy I found seeing the only car in the parking lot was yours. I worried about you walking on the beach alone. You could fall, or I don't know, I was just worrying about you. Imagine how I felt when I called your name and you did not answer me."

Lynette whispered, "I did not hear you. I smelled hot chocolate and wanted to drink some, but I didn't have any money on me."

"I know, I know. I was standing almost beside you drinking hot chocolate. My love, let's go somewhere, just you and me."

Lynette sat down on the bench, saying, "No one is here but you and me. We could shout, and no one would hear us." She did not want to leave him.

Jay sat down across from her, with wild thoughts racing through his mind. He blurted out, "I am here to stay. I tried to sell the assets of my family trust share to my family, but my sister refused to accept my decision. Instead, she will now be the one in charge. I will go along with whatever decision she makes, good or bad."

"Jay, are you saying you want to be with me?"

"Yeah, can I have your permission to court you?" Jay was now laughing in his funny snickering way that once she thought he was making fun of her.

Lynette explained all about the senior travel club. She had a travel mate. Her heart seemed to stop when she heard, "Can you exchange your travel mate for me?"

Lynette ran around the table to Jay giving him a hug around his neck almost choking him. "Will you join my travel club? The first trip will be

Saturday. First thing tomorrow, you must go and sign up. Oh, I do want you to be my travel partner."

Jay walked Lynette to her car. At the door, he said, "If you want, I would like to be your partner for life."

Lynette answered, "Yes, yes!" She silently said a prayer of thanks to God for all the gifts she has received, especially for giving her Jay.

The End